I0543086

CONTENTS

MARK

BROWNING

"There are no actions in this world free from consequences and it is the unforseen that always pose the biggest threat"

LENNOX CORPORATION

Book 1 in The Savior Series

INTRODUCTION

The year is 2146, and it has been 100 years since the fall of the world that once existed. There are many stories told of the times before the collapse when people were free and governments not the corporations ruled the empires. Others will tell you it has been this way since before the collapse. But, the real mystery lies in the collapse itself. The stories range from world war to natural disasters and even the involvement of aliens from another galaxy. They talk of a time when the world was divided by the mighty ocean not surrounded by it; and people were spread out amongst various continents and spoke a variety of intricate languages. No one really knows much about the world before the fall. But, out of the ashes of the old world arose the Lennox Corporation, a ruthless industrial machine disguised as the savior of humanity.

After the fall, humanity was at an all-time low in both population and resources, out of the blue the Lennox Corporation arrived on the scene with a plan to salvage the remaining resources and people to rebuild society. They built sanctuary cities where they welcomed survivors, the only rules were that you provide a blood sample and agree to your assigned work duties. With the world in shambles and people seeking any kind of stability, survivors flocked to these cities in waves eager to flee the chaos of the outside world, and the Lennox Corporation was eager to provide the solution. As time passed, more people showed up. Lennox Corp ran out of room and began taking only the most intelligent and useful human beings into their cities. They even began replacing existing members of their new society with more capable people banishing those deemed unworthy back to the outside world. There are rumors of 100's of people with special cognitive abilities being taken to the city only to disappear. There is no way to know the truth. The only way in is you having something they want, or better yet need .

The outskirts of their new society became the slums, and the world rebuilt itself in the image of the Lennox Corporation. I was born in the slums of sanctuary city 3. My mother died in childbirth and I never knew my father. I have been inside the city only once and that is when they tested me as a child. Rumor is, they are no longer looking for people to live within the cities; however they are testing people from the slums for special cognitive abilities. Many people believe the areas outside of the cities contains contaminants left over from a chemical war that helped lead to the fall. The cities themselves are self-contained and have an independent ecosystem from the outside world surrounding them. These cities are a paradise on an otherwise scorched Earth, controlling everything from food production to medication. When you live in the slums, you scavenge the Wasteland or work for Lennox Corporation in the underground operations. All people in the slums and the cities are micro-chipped. The micro-chips serve to track people, designate their job position and allow them to make purchases with just a scan. People who live in the city have a special code in their microchip allowing them access the city. If you don't live in the city, you don't enter the city without a special pass.

Lennox Corp has several mining and scavenging operations throughout the areas that lie outside of the city beyond the slums. They delegate work daily based on an ability and dependability merit system, but really it's just based on bribes and corruption. Thousands of desperate workers line up every day hoping to make a wage. Every day, the same guys get picked. It's a joke. The rest of the inhabitants of the slums scavenge, steal, and run small trade businesses to survive. Most are chasing the most impossible dream of all and that is admittance into one of Lennox Corps sanctuary cities. There are constant smuggling operations and people trying to bribe their way in. Some have tried purchasing old identities of dead citizens.

The city itself is a very different story. If you live within the city walls, you work for one of three branches of Lennox Corp: Security, Technology, or Production. As stated before, you are micro-chipped and accounted for at all times, even if you leave the city for the night to visit your favorite hooker in the slums. Within the city walls there are no families, few children, no relationships just the tasks they assign you. But their payment to you is clean air, security, luxurious accommodations, top quality food and pretty much any other little extra you desire. The downside of that lifestyle is the loss of human connection, which drives many of the citizens of the city to the slums looking for that interaction they desire. It is very dangerous to have wants in the slums. Everyone is looking to capitalize on any opportunity, especially one that involves a citizen from the city. I can't say that I blame people for robbing. Intimidating citizens was never for me. In this world you do what you can to get by, let the rest sort itself out. My heart always belonged to the Wasteland. There is an entire world of history and treasure to be discovered out there. You just have to survive the fall out and nomadic tribes. The roving tribes are prone to steal and they kill everything they come across. Most have not covered nearly the area that I have in my searches, but I started going out into the Wasteland 23 years ago when I was only 10 with a Nomad named Kalil. Early on, I differed from other human beings. Once, while out exploring with Kalil, a pack of wild dogs attacked me and I sustained what should have been catastrophic injuries. Kalil took me back to our camp to treat my wounds, and I healed fully in only 4 days. After the revelation of those 4 days, Kalil and I decided that it would be better to hide my gifts given the Lennox Corps interest in all things deemed special. As time passed, I only got stronger and my healing abilities became more rapid, making me an extremely effective scavenger in the Wasteland. I now have my niche; people in the slums and in the city know that if they are looking for a rare item, I am their best bet to find it. My name is Tristan, and my home is the Wasteland.

CHAPTER 1

The Job

After spending the winter in an underground bunker that I repossessed from a nomad group that was targeting people traveling between S.C. 2 and S.C. 3, I returned to the slums of S.C. 3 to cash in on a surplus of goods. The winter had been very productive. I had gathered everything from precious metals to hand woven quilts from the Old World. As I approached the slums, I noticed some interesting changes, there were new and much more aggressive Lennox propaganda banners and there was also graffiti opposing the Lennox Corp plastered everywhere. The people versus Lennox Corp must have intensified during my time away. The slums were always one bad day away from erupting and today I felt something a little off. I quickly chalked it up to my ever growing paranoia. Spending so much time alone in the Wasteland had that effect on even the strongest man.

I made my way to Larry's shop to sell my winter's bounty and hopefully be able to trade for a couple of books from the Old World. I had not found a single book all winter. Despite my successful haul, an element of disappointment lingered. If you were in the slums where I grew up and looking to trade or sell goods Larry's shop was the only place to get a decent deal while also securing privacy. Larry had deep connections to people in every slum and his reach even extended into S.C. 3. I entered Larry's shop and he lit up like a solar storm on an October night in the Wasteland. I had never seen him so happy to see me. Though we went way back and I was a good customer, Larry was not the sentimental type. It had to involve a big payday. He invited me into the back, for customers who require discretion, and before I presented my goods, he came right out with it. In a stern, but excited voice he asked me "are you interested in a job with a huge guaranteed payday funded by one of the wealthiest and most influential members of S.C. 3?" I have to admit it intrigued me though doing jobs for citizens was a dangerous game. The last place you want to be is on one of Lennox Corps threat lists. Among the top ways to get there is colluding with or corrupting a citizen of a sanctuary city and throughout all of my activities over the years I have been very selective with my jobs and stayed off their radar. Before I would even consider the job, I told Larry I would need the details and a sit down with the citizen. After the proposition we concluded our business. He paid me a decent amount of credits for my winter stash, but unfortunately he had no books to offer. I did, however, receive an old Road Atlas that shows how travel used to be charted and navigated in the Old World.

As the evening approached and the night life awakened in the slums, I made my way over to Tammy's, the only place that still welcomed me in our slums. Everywhere else deemed me a threat to business because of my bad temper and dislike for the alcohol impaired. Not Tammy though, as I had saved her brother's life when he got lost in the Wasteland and she has always had a room for me since. No one that wants a problem comes around her place. They are well aware it's protected by me, present or not. I will repay any harm visited on her or her establishment ten times over. Tammy was excited to see me, but I had already had my fill of small talk for the evening with Larry so I greeted her politely and then immediately headed for my room. I needed to sleep and have all of my senses working at optimal efficiency to-morrow when I met this mysterious citizen offer-ing a too good to be true job. You never knew what

Lennox Corp was trying to do. Being able to recognize their undercover security agents was a good
way to stay one step ahead of them.

I stopped by to see Larry the next morning, and he informed me that the citizen agreed to
meet me here at the shop that evening at ten, and
he was prepared to offer a fair sum for this mystery job. With time to kill, I spent my day taking
care of some business around the slums. I needed
to go by the scrap yard and see if the blacksmith
had made my climbing spikes. I had scouted
several locations that would require some advanced climbing techniques to reach. The harder
and more dangerous a location was to reach, the
higher the likelihood of it containing anything of
value. One of the things I respect most about the
blacksmith, he only trades in goods and services;
he doesn't accept any Lennox credits. He believes
the Lennox Corporation created credits as another form of control, and he is right.

Kalil told me stories, as a young man growing up, about the times before Lennox Corp took over and how they said they sealed all deals in blood and survival of the fittest ruled the Wasteland. There were no rules and no one to enforce them if there had been. There was only wasteland and failed pop up town after failed pop up town. Lennox Corp provided stability, a currency system and rules for the masses to live by. As for those that didn't want to take part, they were left behind in the Wasteland to fend for themselves. This was before they began turning away people, before the slums or cognitive testing. A time when men like Kalil, Nomads and lone warriors against the world, with no affiliations, ruled the day. As a kid I loved his stories. Those times always sounded like true freedom to me. That is why I loved being out in the Wasteland so much, it was just me against the world.

When I arrived at the blacksmith's scrap

yard, a strange woman with a severe burn scar on her face came to the gate. After giving me a thorough questioning, she finally let me in and introduced herself as Laura the blacksmith's apprentice. She said she and the blacksmith had been in a fire and that he had died. She was lucky to have escaped with her life. Apparently the blacksmith had been working on a special buggy for a group of hijackers who had been working a hilly part of the Wasteland. When they refused to pay, he locked down the yard and kept their buggy. Later that evening, the hijackers returned and burned the blacksmith and Laura out taking the buggy and a surplus of valuable scrap, then disappearing into the Wasteland. Laura told me that their clan wore the logo of the serpent. The logo was all I needed. They could count on a visit from me once I headed back out into the Wasteland.

After a short conversation with Laura she handed me my new climbing spikes. She had made them herself. Evidently, all the old man talked about was our conversations over the years. His last request to her was that she always take care of me first, starting with my climbing spikes. It moved me knowing his last thoughts were of our friendship. I was the only one left alive that knew his actual name. I never told a soul and I never will. May his identity remain a secret in his next life, as well. I left out for the general store to stock up for supplies. I would need plenty of protein paste and dried meat for this next trip.

The blacksmith's death was weighing on my mind. I was heading back into the Wasteland soon; citizen job or not. I had a date with some serpents and two new locations to scavenge now that I had my climbing spikes. I returned to Tammy's, packed up all of my supplies and prepared everything to load into my crawler, a dune buggy built especially for me by the blacksmith. He installed a technology used by Lennox Corp that will only allow me to operate it. The blacksmith had a way of turning machine and tech into one harmonious creature. After loading the crawler, I still had a few hours to kill and decided I'd play cards in Tammy's lounge for a bit. By the time it was time to go meet the citizen, I was down 200 credits and over it, anyway. Cards were never my strength. I wasn't much for games; I preferred things that were more physical in nature; but that came with the territory. If it weren't for Kalil, I would have never learned to read. Now I am always searching out books for the knowledge. I learned about strategy when all I knew was survival; I learned compassion when all I knew was chaos. These concepts and so many more would have eluded me if I had not learned to read. 9 out of 10 people in the slums cannot read past the level of basic comprehension and that is another form of control that they allow Lennox Corp to have over them. The information is there for them, they just don't care to use it. Just another example of why I spend most of my time in the Wasteland. My goal was to be heading out soon.

Having arrived at Larry's about an hour early, I took the opportunity to browse any new inventory he might have picked up overnight, and I was glad I did! There on the counter, right in front of me, laid a book on horticulture that some-one had traded for a measly 75 credits. Believe me when I tell you, I was more than happy to pay Larry 100 credits and add the book to my growing collection. That would mean a stop by my true home, a bunker in the Wasteland buried deep be-neath the fallen structures of the Old World. I kept all of my most valuable possessions there includ-ing an arsenal of weaponry I had been building for over 5 years. The manufacturing of weapons fell under the umbrella of production for Len-nox Corp, but in reality weapon sales was a large funding contributor to the entire operation. The Wasteland is a dangerous place and people need to protect themselves.

Soon after I purchased my most recent book from Larry, a tall slender man with an odd way about him came through the entrance. I could already tell by his appearance, this was my citizen, so I waved him over and introduced myself. It was obvious he had been to the slums before, but he still seemed nervous and agitated. As he introduced himself he kept fidgeting. Mike was the name he gave, though I'm pretty sure it was not his actual name. He explained that while he was in the slums visiting a friend, which usually meant a hooker, a valuable piece of technology was taken from him. If Lennox Corp were to find out he had taken it, he would be fired from his position in the tech division and banished to the slums. He offered to pay me 250,000 credits. His eyes said that was negotiable. I would need to track down and find this piece of lost tech. I asked myself what is worth such a hefty price. Knowing I wouldn't receive the truth from him anyway, I instead asked for the specific size and weight of the object. Taken off guard, the citizen answered my question with a very simple response, "It's a thumb drive and I need it back now." I thought about it in an uncomfortable silence for a few minutes even though I already knew that I would take the job. With 250,000 credits I could stock the bunker for life. I accepted the deal under one condition, he had to write everything down that happened that night and I meant everything, no lies, and no half truths. He gave me a detailed description of the night he lost the drive and I returned to Tammy's pouring through his account of that evening for clues. I had some ideas, but I needed to get some rest. My hope was this would be an easy payday.

CHAPTER 2

Retracing Steps

The citizen was clear and concise; a well-educated man. He stated he had come into town that evening to see a friend, to my surprise, a man called "Big" Tom. I didn't know him personally, but had heard of him. People say he is a whiz on computers and pretty handy at fixing just about anything that has to do with Lennox Corp tech. It made sense that the two of them would be friends seeing as how the citizen worked in the Lennox Corps tech branch. The two had been friends as children and the citizen tested higher than "Big" Tom, therefore Mike grew up within the city walls. But the two stayed friends. They would get together and bounce around new technology ideas and shoot the shit about life in general. Mike said, it was like any night between the two of them; a couple of drinks and a few laughs. But when he presented Tom with the thumb drive and showed him what he had been working on, Tom became furious with him and freaked out. Evidently, Tom told Mike he should never have shown him classified Lennox Corp tech. If they caught the two of them with it, they would toss their bodies out into the Wasteland pit for the buzzards. Mike knew Tom was probably right, but he really needed to talk to somebody he could trust. Tom wanted no part of it though, so Mike said he headed on out. Feeling woozy from the drinks and the adrenaline from the altercation, Mike said he staggered towards the citizen's entrance to the city. This is a notorious area for armed robberies against citizens. Citizens are easy prey before they reach the safety of the transition zone, where they must be scanned to gain admittance into the city. Mike thought 2 men were following him almost as soon as he left Tom's place But later thought he must be paranoid. He had made this walk dozens of times before and never had an issue. Why would tonight be any different? The men approached him walking hastily, pushing almost through him, but never stopped or said a word. It was only upon his return home, he reached in to empty his pockets and found the thumb-drive gone. It must have been a pick pocket. Having finished his story, I knew my next step.

I headed to Big Tom's to see if he had anything to add to the story and get his corroboration of the events as retold by Mike. I didn't want to go to Big Tom empty handed. I asked around and found out that Big Tom was a hoarder of copper wiring or anything that even had copper in it. It just so happened, I had taken a small spool of copper wiring off the nomads that donated their bunker to me for the winter. Trading goods for information definitely speeds up the process. This case was already too much trouble. I had only been back in the slums for 2 days and I was ready to head back out into the Wasteland. The stench of depression and defeat filled the people of the slums. They wore desperation like a ball and chain unable to free themselves from a repetitive cycle of oppression. I could feel the weight of the slums pushing down on me every time I came here. I wanted to help, but I knew there was nothing I could do for them. Even if they made the decision to rebel, Lennox Corp would crush them and start over. Though I am seemingly indestructible, if Lennox Corp found out about my gifts, they would imprison me and condemn me to lifelong experimentation.

When I arrived at Big Tom's house, the entire place was trashed and Big Tom had been beat to shit! Helping him up was a chore even for me.

I now could see firsthand why they called him Big Tom. Tom clearly wasn't one of the starving people. I helped him into an upright sitting position and started trying to coax him back into reality. He was in shock and kept saying something about the special division. If he was talking about the special division of Lennox Corps security branch, we had a genuine problem. That meant they were looking for the drive and Lennox Corp had already discovered Mike's betrayal. Mike was most certainly already dead. Big Tom passed out again after his incoherent rant. I stuck around a bit longer and waited for him to wake up. I still needed information even if it was just to cover my own ass. If Lennox Corp was looking to question anyone involved, I could very well be next on their list. This was not the first time I had seen an example of how they ask questions.

After a few hours, Big Tom woke up, and I was right there copper in hand ready to play the good guy. I didn't want him thinking I was another Lennox Corp goon. Hesitant at first, he finally let me help him up. We made our way to the sink and cleaned up his cuts. I took this opportunity to explain how I came to be there. Tom excepted the copper coil, and we talked for about an hour. He told me that Mike was very upset about a technology he developed some years ago. He seemed very afraid of how Lennox Corp may be using it. Tom immediately told Mike to go home and never come back. Big Tom said that when Mike left the residence, he knew the trouble they were in. Tom said he refused to see what Mike had on the thumb drive; he didn't want to know. Tom's fears were justified; 2 days later members of Lennox Corps top security unit showed up and beat Big Tom nearly to death. They tore his entire place apart looking for the drive. To my advantage, this meant they didn't know where it was either.

Mike's hunch about a pick pocket must have

been right. I hung around Big Tom's until nightfall and retraced Mike's steps back to the transition area to see if I noticed any of the usual suspects working the area. I walked the drag all night and though I saw my fair share of illicit activities, mostly con artists and beggars, but I saw no pick pockets. I obviously wasn't leaving the slums tonight. I had no leads and no ideas. As I approached Tammy's, I noticed something wasn't right. There was no one hanging around outside, and an eerie quiet hung over the entire area. My senses never fail me. As I entered, an entire room full of Special Division agents from Lennox Corp. sat waiting for me. After seeing how they handled Big Tom, and knowing that they had a special knack for finding violence in even the most calm situation, I decided it best to enter calmly and immediately lay face down on the floor. An altercation with these men would be sure to expose my gifts. The man in charge granted me permission to get up and join him at the table for a business proposition. He introduced himself as Special Division Commander for S.C. 3. The commander told me they were well aware of my business arrangement with Mike. The commander explained that he was well informed of the people and activities in S.C. 3, and that it seems I have somewhat of a legend status here in the slums. But the way he said it, with a note of sarcasm, believe me, he was not impressed. The commander said, "We want to hire you to find the Lennox Corp thumb drive. Mike is no longer available to work with you. You would be working for me. This won't be a problem will it?" What could I say? He said they had information that a small time pick pocket had stolen the drive. When he couldn't break the code, he sold it to a hacker group that appeared to be taking it to the slums of S.C. 1. We think they have a bunker somewhere around there. Lennox Corp is prepared to transfer 50,000 credits to your account, half right away half when you retrieve the drive. I wasn't normally one to have anything to do with

Lennox Corp, but in my mind the job just got easier with better guarantees. I now had valuable information about who had the drive and I was being paid by the corporation, including half up front; I agreed. This was definitely better than being thrown into a pit in the Wasteland wasting away under circling buzzards. I can only assume that would have been my fate. It was clear they needed this drive, and they wanted to keep it quiet. With my reputation and connections in the slums, they figured I could get more information from the locals. The situation suited me just fine. The sooner this job was done, the sooner I could leave. My eagerness to head back to the Wasteland was growing by the day.

My quick payday was leading me into unfamiliar territory. I had been nowhere near S.C. 1 in over 10 years. After accepting the job, I couldn't help but think about Mike. I knew he was dead, but I didn't feel bad for him because for him this was the only way things could have turned out. I should have told him he could never go back to the city. From the moment I met him I knew his fate. As I tried to get my head back in the game, I realized the commander was giving me a detailed file on the hacker group. They called themselves Cloud 9 and had been a pain in the ass of Lennox Corp for years. They stayed very mobile and had operatives in all three slums. Many believed they had moles inside the city itself. Something Lennox Corp would fully deny. I was very familiar with this group of hackers, but I played dumb. In my experience, I had found that the best way to get information out of people was to play dumb and let them do the talking. If you intimidate them with your intelligence, they close up and become threatened by you. It's always better to let them feel in control. Cloud 9 was traveling to S.C. 1 with five paid mercenaries as protection, which meant they would have to stop at the trading post for the night. The trading post was 3 days from here, and then it was another 4 days to S.C. 1. If you were willing to cut through Serpent territory, you could get to the trading post in just over a day and a half. It just so happened that not only was I willing to cut through Serpent territory, I insisted. I had a score to settle. I intended to make sure that no one dared call themselves a Serpent ever again.

I had a small cache of weapons hidden away just outside of the slums. Those would have to do for now. I had no time to return to my bunker. The Serpents were more like a cult than anything else. You could ask any member of the group their name and they would all respond one word "Snake". But I knew something that few knew. I knew who the head of the Serpents was, a man named Waylon. He grew up in the same area of the Slums as I did. Though only a few years older than I, he had a fierce reputation as a killer. Waylon disappeared into the Wasteland for a few years and returned with a small following of hijackers calling themselves the Serpents. They soon grew to over 30 members and now control a crucial stretch of the Wasteland. Their primary drive is to rob and kill travelers. They have collected a lot of mechanical parts throughout the years and built themselves a rolling convoy of top notch vehicles for road warfare. I had contemplated many strategies of destruction for the Serpents over the years, but it was time to make a plan and execute it. The Serpents had slithered around in my Wasteland long enough. I waited until well after dark and headed out. I had learned that the wild dogs had poor eyesight and didn't hunt at night so that was when I did most of my traveling. They couldn't kill me, but their attacks were violent and relentless. I preferred to avoid them at all costs.

CHAPTER 3

Snake Wrangler

I made my way out of the slums to retrieve my cache, my mind working on how I would kill 30 plus serpents in armored vehicles. Sometimes in life the toughest questions answer themselves. When I opened up the box containing my cache, clarity came. Not only had I stashed some decent weaponry, I had also stashed improvised explosive devices. I intended to use the explosives to blow open an old mining tunnel that I found on an Old World map. The removal of the Serpents would be a much better use. I decided the ultimate tribute to the blacksmith would be to rig explosives to the buggy he built for me and drive right into their convoy, blowing them all straight to the depths of the Wasteland. I was the only one equipped for this job; I had survived being blown up 3 times! I knew for a fact that I would not only survive but would only require about 6 hours of down-time to heal. By my calculations, that still put me at the trade station well ahead of Cloud 9.

I rigged up my buggy and rode for Serpent territory. As I thought it out, first the exterior patrols would need to be taken out. Second, I had to lure out the convoy and trigger the explosion. Waylon drove the lead truck nicknamed the "Hard Charger", a modified tow truck built to ram and clear paths for their artillery trucks. They mounted these trucks with 50 caliber rifles and harpoons. Blindsiding Waylon would be the only way to set off the explosion. If he hits me and opens me up to their artillery vehicles, things would get messy quick. The last thing I wanted was some Serpent escaping during a firefight and telling everyone in the slums he saw me take damage from heavy artillery, without as much as slowing me down. This had to be a clean sweep, no one walks away.

I headed out to the edge of Serpent territory and, like clockwork, the first patrol appeared. In about five minutes, the next patrol came along. I stashed the buggy a little over a mile away and made my way over to their patrol loop on foot. I waited for one of them to pass again and give me my five minute window. I snuck out into the middle of the highway and lay down like a drunk-ard passed out. The patrol approached quickly, slowing only as they came upon my still body in the road. They shined their spotlight on me and took up a position, waiting for the other patrol to circle around and join them. I had found the perfect position to take the advantage. Taking out both patrols should be easy. Once the other patrol arrived to provide backup, the four men all surrounded me. Now they were out of their vehicles and exposed. Just a little closer now and I will strike. One man came near and poked me with his rifle barrel. I made a swift move grabbing the barrel, and rolling over removed the weapon from his grasp. I fired multiple shots into his midsection. His lifeless body fell to the ground. The other men raised their weapons and started firing! Each shot that landed burned a little more than the last one. I had become so accustomed to taking gunfire; I healed almost as fast as the bullets hit these days. My body continued to absorb the shots as I moved from target to target removing each one's throat with my bare hands. These men did not deserve honorable deaths! They will tell no stories in the afterlife.

The convoy will have heard the shots and be gearing up for a fight. I would use the speed and handling of the buggy to get into position. The key would be to hit them quick and hard be-

fore those artillery vehicles opened fire. I heard
the rumble of the convoy pushing fast towards
my position, so I looped around and set up on
the flank. I threw the road flares as I pulled the
buggy around. I wanted there to be as much confusion as possible. The road flares were working.
The convoy decreased their speed. As they approached the ambush area, I gunned the buggy and
headed down the side of the hill, gaining speed
as I descended on the convoy. As I sped towards
them, I misjudged my approach and hit the second
vehicle, not Waylon. Next came the flash; a beautiful explosion of Serpents and metal! However,
this joy did not come without a cost. The pain
of the explosion was unbearable. The last thing I
remember was the smell of scorched and burning
flesh. A few hours later I woke up good as new just
like I always do. The only side effect, as always,
was that I woke up foggy and struggling to remember what happened. Thankfully, this doesn't
usually last long. I looked around at the vast de-

struction and took a moment to enjoy my victory. My buggy had served its purpose. This had been a long time coming.

As I regained my wits, I scavenge around the wreckage for anything that might be useful to me later. I worked my way out to the Serpent's stronghold; anyone left would present minimal resistance. They had abandoned the hideout. Either I had killed everyone, or the rest had bugged out after the explosion. I found everything necessary to head out to the trading post including an old rail buggy. I found Waylon's quarters and it appeared he had bugged out, as well. My mistimed hit might mean Waylon could still be alive, and that put me a little on edge. My hope was he was unaware of who executed the hit. If he survived, it wouldn't be long, and he would begin recruiting for the Serpents again, but he will have to find a new residence first. I took everything that I could fit in the buggy. I couldn't be sure what I would need once I reached the trading post. Though not a victory, it would take Waylon a while to rebuild and recruit. So for now, my wasteland is Serpent free, and I am on my way to pick up the biggest score of my life.

The night was crisp, and the air felt lighter knowing that I had avenged the blacksmith and I would finish the job with Waylon. Right now I had a schedule to keep. The trip to the trading post went smooth, and I found myself enjoying the night sky as it reflected strange green and pink hues. It was time to shift my focus to recovering the hard drive.

CHAPTER 4

Fair Trade

As I approached the trading post outside of S.C. 1, it was buzzing with activity. Blending in with the crowd to watch the comings and goings would be easy but I had other business first. I wanted to pick up supplies, a new vehicle and some information on the slums of S.C. 1. I had not been there in a long time, and they operated by a unique set of rules. I had to figure out the best place to hit the security detail protecting the hackers, and it needed to be strategic, not loud. The goal: try not to kill the hackers. Let's face it, without revolutionaries like them, who would expose Lennox Corp. Unfortunately, in this situation they may have bitten off more than they could chew. Their security detail was of no consequence to me. Mercenaries were just fake tough guys too scared of the Wasteland to scavenge, so they make a living playing errand boy for people even more scared than they are. They traveled in teams and always numbered five; never more never less. My first order of business would be collecting information on S.C. 1, so I headed over to the bar.

I sat down at the bar and ordered moonshine and a protein paste. My bill was 50 credits. I gave the bartender 500 credits and played the waiting game. When she returned, she told me to talk to Henry when he came in and the tip will need to be double. At 1000 credits, Henry better be the guy. I slid my moonshine down to the drunk a few stools away. I've never found much use for alcohol. It makes people impaired and impaired people have very bad judgment. I choked down my protein paste and relaxed while I waited for Henry. About an hour later, a short stout man came in and manned the bar. He had a sour demeanor and a no nonsense attitude; this had to be Henry. I sat quietly waiting for him to engage me in conversation.

Kalil had taught me about trading posts at a very young age. He always said, "Everything there is for sale, even your life." I always took that to heart. There is a specific way to conduct business; step out of line and you pay the consequences. When I was 17, Kalil, and I visited a trading post in the fringes when an outlaw nicknamed Grizzly got way out of line, harassing the ladies and running his mouth to anyone who would listen. Though a feared man, you don't mess with trade. The vendors drugged his liquor and that night. When he passed out, they skinned him alive and hung him in the square for everyone to see. I still see the image of his lifeless, skinless body every time I recall the event.

The bartender interrupted my trip down memory lane and as I had done before, I ordered my moonshine but this time tipped him the 1,000 credits. After 20 minutes or so had passed, he invited me to take a smoke break with him out back. I slid my moonshine down to the drunk, gave him a smile and headed out back with Henry. He jumped right to the point, which suited me just fine. I asked my first question, "Who runs the slums?" Being the slums of the first sanctuary city, they built them on the backs of dangerous men that played by their own rules. The slums of S.C. 1 were a melting pot of hardened psychos and top tier criminals. I was looking to avoid them. Our slums were a mix of people from outlaws to families. Kalil and I always made sure no one ran our slums. Many had tried, all had failed. But, Lennox Corp had promised a bonus if I could come up with the buyer and the trick would be gauging the risk versus reward. Do I, for the bonus, let Cloud 9 make it to S.C. 1 and meet with their buyer or do I just hit them in transit, take the thumb drive and collect my original payment?

Henry told me Captain Chip, a scavenger and smuggler, ran S.C. 1. He goes back to when you used tunnels to get in and out of S.C. 1. These tunnels had been dug by the smugglers themselves using only small hand tools and sheer determination. Lennox Corp has since sealed the tunnels and the cities that followed S.C. 1 took preventative measures against all forms of illegal entry. I didn't let on, but the news about Captain Chip was good for me. Captain Chip was a friend of Kalil's and I, we knew him as Charlie. I felt confident I could get whatever necessary from Captain Chip. Now, I can wait until the exchange and hit the buyer for the thumb drive, avoiding casualties to any of the hackers.

The security team is always 5 men, but I wasn't sure how many members of Cloud 9 were making the trip, so I hung out and did a little re-connaissance. Outpacing them to S.C. 1 would be easy and cutting through the salt marshes was an option. Henry gave me an extra tip about the main road to S.C. 1. It seems a group of hijackers known as the Road Men had been working a stretch of the road near an old structure that had collapsed. I knew the spot he was talking about; they had picked a perfect place for an ambush. I had to get ahead of Cloud 9 and clear that threat. I didn't need those mercenary clowns getting the Cloud 9 members killed before they made this deal.

I tipped Henry another 500 credits, thanked him and went back inside to post up at the bar. Cloud 9 would arrive soon. The first place the mercenaries would go when they got in to town was the bar. A couple more hours passed, and still no sign of them. I began worrying the mercenaries had gotten lost or worse yet, hijacked. Just as I thought about heading out to secure lodging for the evening, they came staggering in. You could spot these clowns a mile away: overblown tough guys with enormous guns and big mouths. They appeared to be escorting 3 young adults between the ages of 18 and 22. These were definitely my hackers. All 3 carried briefcases used to transport digital interface kits, and only hackers use those. As I expected, the tough guys headed to the bar shortly after their arrival. With the hour so late, they won't be getting an early start. I'll take that advantage.

Now, knowing how many there were in the group, I could head out in the morning and secure those supplies and a new mode of transportation. I waved Henry over and asked him the best place to stay. I already had an idea of where to stay, but if Henry made the call and hooked it up for me, I might save a few credits. As I had hoped, he slipped me a card with a name on it, told me to hand it to the lady at the pink house and not to worry about payment, his treat. I thanked him yet again and made my way through the square to the pink house, a well-known and very popular brothel. I just wanted the bed. Hopefully, they wouldn't care if I passed on the girl since she is paid up. I knocked on the door and showed the doorman the card. He showed me in and introduced me to a beautiful red-haired, green-eyed woman with legs for days. I handed her the card, and she showed me to the room. I explained my appreciation for Henry's generosity, but for now I told her I wanted some privacy and rest. She seemed reluctant to leave as she turned to head out but made sure I knew she was available if I changed my mind.

I got up early and headed out to the square. I still had to purchase some kind of transportation. Supplies like protein paste and jerky were easy to come by, but vehicle selection could be limited and expensive. When I approached the mechanic's shop, I was surprised to see it closed considering the 24 hours a day 7 days a week policy the trade vendors followed. I tried to look into the front window, but as I did, I heard screams coming from the garage area. I kicked the office door in and ran towards the back to investigate the screams. I entered the garage to see the mechanic strung up and severely burned and tortured. Around him stood four men with machetes and long dark coats, each one dressed alike. I said "Can I maybe have a word with the mechanic about the trail bike I spotted out back before you guys kill him?" One man spoke up, "Take the bike and get out!" I have to admit, for a second I thought to myself, a free motorcycle would be nice, but there is always a price. Even doing nothing costs something. I lunged forward at the one who had spoken, separating his shoulder and running him through with his own blade. I reached down, pulled out the throwing knife from my boot and flung it across the room, planting it into the neck of the next man. Before I made my next move, the two remaining men retreated with incredible speed leaving the mechanic's shop. I cut the mechanic down and carried him to the couch. I found some water, antiseptic and bandages. I hollered out into the square, "I need a nurse! Is anyone a nurse?" A woman approached me but said it would cost me 150 credits. I told her I didn't have that much, but I felt sure the men inside would have plenty. I didn't mention they were dead. She agreed and followed me back to the garage. After she patched the mechanic up, she asked me, "Where are the men who are supposed to pay me? I pointed at the dead men lying in the floor. To my surprise, she walked over and scanned the dead men for their credits, and left seemingly thrilled. As the mechanic had finally calmed down, I asked about the trail bike I wanted to purchase and he simply responded, "It's yours." I wanted to pay him, but he said we had already struck a deal, and his life for the price of a motorcycle seemed a fair trade. With transportation taken care of, I gathered supplies and set off for the collapsed structure along the road to S.C. 1 where the Road Men should be set up. Hopefully with a little recon and a quick solution I can have the path cleared for Cloud 9 and they will be none the wiser.

CHAPTER 5

Guardian Angel

The area that the Road Men held made for a natural choke point, with a marsh on each side forcing vehicles to funnel in through a small area along a 4 mile stretch. You know they were making a killing. I needed to stash my bike about 2 miles away and make the push on foot to do my recon. I refused to lose my sweet new bike. I had only had it a few hours. I found a perfect place to stash it. Once I secured it, I struck out on foot to recon the Road Men's camp and the stretch where they set up the roadblock. I might draw them out by blowing up the road-block and creating a diversion big enough to get the drop on them. I knew little of the Road Men never having run into them in the past. The information that I received about them suggested they hadn't been in the area long. There would always be those seeking to take advantage of the weak. I rarely considered myself a code of ethics guy, but I believe in trying to do what's right and always letting your conscience be your guide. Most people didn't even understand what that meant, which helps to explain the state of the world.

I approached the camp from the south. It worked last time, so I again mustered up my best drunkard routine traveling the road on foot. My intel stated they only attacked groups and vehicles that they consider high value targets. In theory, I should be able to stumble right by and get a look at everything without raising too much suspicion. I slowly walked past their roadside camp observing them as they geared up for a big score. They were readying themselves, probably for the hit on Cloud 9. I continued walking and talking to myself without even one of them as much as raising an eye in my direction. I counted 11 around the camp, well armed and ready for a fight. As I made my way to the roadblock, I quickly realized I would not be using my original plan. I didn't have the materials or the time to blow up such a significant barrier. They posted four more Road Men at the blockade. I decided removing these four from the equation would be where I would start. I stumbled up to the blockade and began throwing a fit screaming and yelling about the blockade keeping me from my daily walk. The men all began laughing as they approached me. I'm sure I appeared the perfect target for some sadistic fun. Today would not be their lucky day. As they approached, I pretended to pull out my manhood and urinate on their blockade, hiding my right hand as I slowly pulled out my hatchet waiting for them to come within striking distance. One of them placed his arm on my shoulder yanking me back away from the blockade. The blade of my hatchet whistled as I drew down and took off his arm in one quick stroke! The other three men stood there frozen in shock as I took them apart. One of them finally raised his hand to block his face as the hatchet gave him a split personality. I drug their bodies out into the marsh for disposal. As I was carrying them down, I realized I could use the marsh to approach the camp from an unprotected vantage point. People were afraid of the marsh. Many believed that there were creatures that lived in there that loved to prey on human beings when given the opportunity. Kalil had taught me the truth through some Old World books. The gasses released by the marshlands causes hallucinations and then people become disoriented, getting lost and eventually consumed. But, if you have a breathing respirator like the ones used for exploring caves and loot sites, you can safely navigate the marshlands. I always kept a respirator on me for exploration and cutting through the marsh.

It was time to get back to the men occupy-
ing the camp. No approach would be easy. I didn't
have time for a long drawn out recovery so I
needed to take as little damage as possible. Once I
finished with the Road Men, I would still need to
clear the blockade to assure safe passage for Cloud
9. Two teams of three patrolled the perimeter and
another team of five was relaxing around the
camp. My plan, isolate each of the smaller patrols
and then move in to finish the rest of the men. I
didn't know which one was the leader and at this
point I didn't care. They would all be deceased
shortly. I made the tough trip around through the
marsh to get a good attack angle on the first patrol.
Precision would be the key. If a weapon fired, I
would lose the element of surprise. My throwing
knives were to be my weapon of choice. I should
be able to take out two in one throw and be on top
of the third guy before he knew what hit him. I settled down into a mud bank, staying low and wait-

ing for the first patrol to pass. As they got a few feet past me, I threw a knife and then quickly a second, before the first two bodies dropped, the third man's neck throbbed in my clutch, choking him out without a sound. I set my sights on the next patrol working an area near the structures closer to the main camp. It wouldn't be as easy taking them out without alerting the others. I noticed, when they went behind the East side of the structure, it obstructed the view from camp. This would be my attack window. I made my move up to the structure and waited. I needed to catch them as soon as they turned the corner. I waited in anticipation and as soon as they turned the corner I grabbed the first man slamming his head into the wall. I immediately reached to the throat of the second man and followed with the temple of the third sending them all to their maker without a peep. I picked up one of their rifles. With the other men gathered around the fire, this would be easy pickings. I scoped in on the first, putting my first

shot directly in his head. I immediately rotated
and fired on the second target hitting him in the
neck. The other three men tried to return fire, but
I already changed my position to eliminate another target. I had the last two pinned down in the
bushes. I pushed on to the one on my left giving
myself a good look at a shot landing one to his
upper chest caving his entire body. The last man
tried to make a run for it. He made it about 120
yards before I got a clear shot and dropped him.

The only thing left to do now was search
the location for something to blow or clear that
blockade. I searched all the tents and old structures in the area and found nothing capable of
blowing up the barricade. And then there in the
distance, an old big rig that might plow through
the blockade. I read an interesting book from the
Old World about big rigs being the lifeline of the
supply trade back then. These days they used
them to make enormous vehicles for running over

top of smaller vehicles and to carry several men with large arsenals. I jumped in and after a few frustrating minutes trying to get it started, it finally turned over. I needed to build up as much speed as possible to punch through the blockade. My adrenaline spiked as the vehicle picked up speed and I approached the barricade. And then, like a symphony of twisted metal, I punched through the barricade compromising the entire structure clearing the way for Cloud 9.

I would make camp just out of sight in the marsh. I needed to tail them moving forward making sure there were no more surprises along the way. I returned to my bike and made my way to an observation point that would allow me to see them pass. Cloud 9 and the team would see the chaos but hopefully it wouldn't touch off any alarms with the security team. I laid low in the marsh for a few hours while I waited for Cloud 9 to pass. I passed the time setting traps for swamp rats and checking them periodically. In the slums, swamp rat meat was worth a lot of money, though I never really cared for it; too greasy. The first hour drew a catch of zero, but on the third pass I caught 6 rats out of 10 traps making for a decent catch. I skinned and cleaned the rats getting them ready for sale. I packaged the meat and packed up my gear. The time was getting near for Cloud 9 to pass and I needed to be ready to be mobile. Finally, Cloud 9 and their security team passed through and I followed a little ways behind them just out of the range of detection.

The next stretch of road between here and S.C. 1 was safe as far as road bandits, but the wild dogs did most of their hunting here. Wild dogs would kill anything except another wild dog, making their packs strong, loyal, and huge. Wild dogs were the alpha predator of the Wasteland because of their cooperation within the pack, and the main reason I usually avoided S.C. 1. About

15 miles past the Road Men's camp, I realized my biggest fear; a large dog pack tracking the Cloud 9 convoy from the depths of the marsh. I didn't have time to deal with a pack of wild dogs. I would need to cut into the marsh and get out ahead of them, shifting their focus to me. Baiting the pack into chase should lead them away from Cloud 9. There was a bridge about 5 miles up. If I could lead the pack far enough away, the Cloud 9 convoy would have time to clear the bridge and they would be safe. It was time to see what my new bike could do. I pulled back on the throttle and headed into the marsh staying to the mud packs and avoiding the deeper holes. I took a direct intercept path with the front of the dog pack to draw the attention of the lead dog. As I came up on the left front of the pack, I saw the lead dog eyeing me so I hit a steep mud pack jumping the bike over the lead dog and heading off into the marsh. The lead dog gave chase, and the rest of the pack followed. I led them on a chase through the marsh, finally losing

them after a few minutes of white knuckle rid-
ing. I doubled back around and picked up my tail
on Cloud 9. This score better be worth it, otherwise I'm just playing Guardian Angel for a bunch of
hackers.

CHAPTER 6

Captain Chip

After what probably seemed like smooth sailing to Cloud 9, we all arrived in the slums of S.C. 1 safe and sound. As the hackers sought lodging, the security team, as always, sought out the bar. My information suggested they had a meeting with the buyer 2 days from now, so that would give me plenty of time to talk to Captain Chip and find out where the deal would take place. I hoped to cut him in and get an easy set up to hit the deal and confiscate the thumb drive. The last few days had been exhausting, and I need some rest. Finding Chip and setting up a meeting would have to wait until tomorrow.

The wild dogs haunted my mind and my dreams. Still, I awoke feeling recharged and re-focused though I would have preferred a better night's sleep. Word around town was Captain Chip had a compound of cargo containers on the North side of the slums. He seemed to run everything from there. Unfortunately, I was having a hard time finding a contact to get me in or arrange a meeting with him, so I opted for a direct approach and headed for the front gate. I was hopeful he would remember me. I approached the gate and gave my name to the person on watch letting him know I was here to see Captain Chip. Though we had not seen each other in years, Captain Chip re-membered me immediately and seemed almost excited to see me. Back then he was not in a posi-tion of power; it was obvious he didn't get many friendly guests these days. He immediately began asking me about Kalil, the two of them had been close back in the day. I couldn't tell him it had been years since I had seen Kalil. Everyone in our slums thought he was dead, but I hoped not. Best I could tell, Kalil found a map from the Old World and set out to cross the Wasteland through the infected zone in search of a destination he believed to be a paradise on Earth. So as I thought about it, I told Captain Chip that Kalil was doing great, exploring and scavenging the Wasteland as usual and then steered the conversation in Captain Chip's direction.

I wanted to know how he managed to work himself into such a high level position. It seems, as he explained, "A few years back the organized crime oppression became so bad in S.C. 1 that the citizens of the slums finally rebelled under my command. I brokered a backroom deal with Lennox Corp to provide extra guns and muscle for us to take back the slums. Lennox Corp agreed, but I had to run the slums under their direction." In his eagerness to lead the people of the slums to victory over organized crime, he led them to op-pression under Lennox Corp. Honestly I thought S.C. 1 felt much different from the last time. I saw no illegal activity, and I didn't hear a sound after 2 a.m. These slums were clearly being run by Len-nox Corp and I saw the future of S.C. 2 and S.C. 3 and therefore all the people. This was a concern for an-other time.

Now that Captain Chip had explained his actual role, I was hesitant to tell him about my purpose in the slums. The reality was I couldn't do it without him. I had no knowledge of who the buyer was or where the transaction would go down. I filled him in on my situation and to my surprise he was already aware and expecting me. That explained my warm welcome. Lennox Corp had already filled him in on the situation and advised him to help me in any way possible. He already had all the information on the contact and where the deal would take place. My understanding of the importance of this thumb drive continued to grow, and it had to be a private contractor like me to retrieve it, not a Lennox Corp security team. They didn't need backlash from the slums if things got out of hand with these hackers. Every time the slums get stirred up they revolt and cause mass damage attacking the city's perimeter and destroying supply lines. If I ended up killing a bunch of hackers, I'm just a psycho contractor doing a job. We were to contact someone known as "The Beacon". No one even knew if they were male or female. Lennox Corp had been trying to get a positive identification on this person for months, hence the bonus. I thanked him for the information and headed back to the room to put everything I had learned so far together.

Later that evening, there was a light knock on my door; it was Captain Chip. I invited him in and we sat down at the table where I had been working. He appeared rather apprehensive. I could tell he had something to disclose to me, but I would have never guessed what followed. He got up and checked around the room. After completing the round, he seated himself back at the table. He then said, "Lennox Corp has my entire complex under surveillance. Listen, you can't hit that deal, I'm the Beacon". I couldn't believe what I was hearing. Here I was convinced he was a lackey for Lennox Corp. He continued, "I'm convinced that thumb drive contains the information to shut down the Lennox Corp barge. Supposedly, Lennox Corp had a boat filled with servers anchored offshore; the nervous system for their entire operation. I had heard stories about the barge all my life, but no one could confirm its existence. If this was true, we were involving ourselves in a deadly game. Shutting them down may be the only way to avoid a takeover and implementation of slavery in the slums. He required my help, but I had to think about it. I had prepared myself to get the thumb drive and collect the pay day not to save the world. With those credits, I could strike out across the Wasteland in search of Kalil or paradise, whichever comes first. I thought about it all night long. What we were talking now was next level dangerous. Nearly every plan I came up with involved me helping Captain Chip and Cloud 9. I recognized what I had to do, but this called for a solid strategy. There was no doubt in my mind, Lennox Corp would be prepared and they have no intention of losing.

I decided I would approach Cloud 9 knowing that Lennox Corp was watching Captain Chip. We needed Lennox Corp to believe the hit took place. To do that, we would need to supply them with a dummy thumb drive. While doing recon on Cloud 9, I had noticed a kid that grew up with me in the slums. He was my best contact with Cloud 9. If I remembered correctly they called him Jake. I approached the back of the quarters where they had taken up lodging, knocked on the door and asked for Jake. Not one of their security team was in the area; worthless drunks. A kid answered the door. He couldn't have been over 19. He said "no one has called me Jake since I was a kid, they call me J3 now." He was a little older but I could see the resemblance now. I explained to him I remembered him from when he was just a kid hanging around the blacksmith's shop and garage. He recognized me, and even remembered some stories the Blacksmith and I used to tell. I wanted to take a stroll down memory lane with him, but now was not the time. I interrupted explaining the Cloud 9 team was in immediate danger. He invited me in and I explained that I needed to sit down with whoever was running Cloud 9 right now. To my surprise that same kid, that used to sit there listening to me and the blacksmith, was now the head of one of the most notorious hacker groups known to the slums. I quickly filled J3 in on the situation and he did not disappoint. He said, "I will create a ghost drive that contains all the same information as the real thumb drive. Here's the kicker, it would deteriorate a few hours after activation, erasing itself and allowing us to keep possession of the real thumb drive. The meeting will go as planned and you can show up to spoil the party, stealing the ghost drive."

The only thing left to do was find someone to pretend to be the buyer as to not expose Captain Chip. In a slum, mostly controlled by Lennox Corp, it was too dangerous to go out looking for someone up to the task. We would need Captain Chip to set that up and I was going back to his compound next. I had to find a way to let him in on the plan without exposing ourselves to Lennox Corp. He had mentioned to me he only trusted one person, his personal bodyguard. A note slipped to him should get to Captain Chip. I showed up for our official meeting and went over the details of my plan to steal the thumb drive. I would bust in as the exchange was being made and confiscate the drive, then drag the buyer out into the street and hold his face up to the Lennox Corp drone. They should be flying over head and this will give them their identification verification. Whoever Captain Chip chose had better be loyal and strong. It won't take long after the identification to pick him up, and he will face a brutal interrogation. Captain Chip and I confirmed the timeline and I slipped the note to his bodyguard, containing the actual plans, on my way out. This was all I could do. The wheels were now in motion. I knew the layout of the building where the deal was taking place, and the mercenaries would offer little resistance as they had been drinking for 2 days straight. If I navigated the building properly, I could enter the room where the deal was taking place without being detected by those goons.

We set the meeting for 11 p.m. and I made my way in shortly after. I easily snuck past the mercenaries and through the building to the meeting room. I came in and there was J3 and a couple members of Cloud 9 along with Captain Chip's guy, a hard looking man with a chip on his shoulder. I asked him if he understood the ramifications of the decision he was making and he acknowledged that he was well aware and wanted to take as much away from Lennox Corp as they had taken away from him. After this was over I needed more information about what had been going on at S.C. 1 and its slums. If Lennox Corp's planned on mandating this new approach across all slums, I needed to prepare and warn the people of the other slums. As we finished, I took possession of the ghost drive and drug Captain Chip's man out into the street for drone identity verification. Once the drone scanned him, he just waited there for Lennox Corp forces to show up and take him into custody.

Later that evening, I met with the commander of the Lennox Corp security division. He had been back in town at S.C. 1 waiting for me to contact him. I turned over the ghost drive and just as promised he transferred the 50,000 credits plus my bonus, to my account and we parted ways. Something felt a little too easy but all I could think about now was the two-hour window before the data on the drive would start breaking down. I needed to get out of S.C. 1 fast! I had already suggested J3 and Cloud 9 disappear immediately after the deal goes down. This would give them a head start. I was hoping to catch up to them quickly down the road and accompany them back to the S.C. 3 slums. This whole incident gave them cause to fire the security team, and I had now volunteered to escort them across the Wasteland back to S.C. 3. Once we arrive back in the S.C. 3 slums, J3 can hack the thumb drive deeper and pull out more information. We needed to know what we were working with, and now that Captain Chip has helped provide the actual thumb drive, it should be an easy task for J3 to pull all the information so I can start planning our attack.

CHAPTER 7

Hidden Danger

The trip to S.C. 3 was uneventful and I couldn't have been happier. Now all we had to do was sneak J3 and Cloud 9 to their underground bunker on the East side of the slums. The bunker made a great hideout as everyone thought the area had been decimated by bunker bombs some years ago. Even if some knew of the bunker, the people loved Cloud 9 and would never tell. All that said, we still had to lie low. By now, Lennox Corp would know the drive was a fake and be looking harder than ever for Cloud 9. However, that would change quickly if they saw me with the Cloud 9 members. We all maneuvered through the street avoiding eye contact and, found our way to their East side bunker. Now at the bunker, Cloud 9 would be safe and J3 could focus on breaking the thumb drive pass code. Thinking I was in the clear, I made my way back to the slums. Lennox Corp would be on the hunt and I had to find out if I was on their radar. I made my way over to Tammy's and checked into my room for some much-needed rest. If Lennox Corp was looking for me, it wouldn't be long before they showed up. All I knew was I had to get some damn sleep. In the morning, I would check in with some of my contacts. Let's hope my name isn't coming up anywhere.

The first thing on the agenda, check in with Laura the blacksmith. I planned to spend a nice chunk of my newly acquired credits with her. She smiled gently and seemed pleased to see me. She had been busy fabricating me an amazing grappling hook, lightweight and durable to pair with my climbing spikes. I could now get into some of those hard-to-reach places I had scoped out in the Wasteland. She tried not to charge me, but I insisted and paid her 1,000 credits. I asked her if she had heard any new news lately. She said Lennox Corp had increased their presence in town the last couple days. They apparently were looking for anyone with information on Cloud 9. I took it as a good sign that she didn't mention anything about me. While we were talking, I informed Laura of the demise of the Serpents. They would no longer pose a threat to her or the shop I assured her. I could immediately see in her eyes, a huge weight had lifted. She thanked me profusely, and as she hugged me, I felt myself give way and I hugged her, too. There was something about her; I just couldn't put my finger on it yet. I knew when I was around her, I felt calm. Well, introspection on that would have to wait.

My next stop was to talk to Larry and see what news he had from the slums. I not only had some trading to do, but I was still hoping I would find some decent books. As I was leaving Laura's, I ran into the Special Commander, now a very familiar face. I thought to myself, this can only mean one thing; they are aware of my involvement and are here to take me in for torture on information involving Cloud 9. I kept thinking this is not acceptable. I would end up exposing my abilities to Lennox Corp and half the slums if this goes bad. The Special Commander approached me, shook my hand and thanked me for the job I had done in the slums of S.C. 1. He then apologized for interrupting my day knowing I had just arrived back. He wanted to hire me for another job and asked if we could set a meeting. My radar went up. Am I really in the clear?! Another job was risky but if I turned it down or refused to listen it could draw suspicion. We agreed to meet in the parlor at Tammy's at 11 in the evening.

After my encounter with the Special Commander, I headed back out for Larry's shop. As I entered, he was very excited to see me. He always knew I had plenty of credits to spend. I asked if any books had come in. Unfortunately there were no books. The news for supply replenishment however was much better. He showed me a tactical knapsack I was very interested in purchasing. I thanked him for always looking after me, transferred 250 credits and headed back to Tammy's with the sack over my shoulder. I wanted to take it easy until it was time to meet with the Special Commander.

Laying there staring at the ceiling, there was no doubt in my mind this job had to do with Cloud 9 and the hard drive deception pulled at the deal in the S.C. 3 slums. I reached over and picked up a book to take my mind off the meeting. When I over think things, I get in trouble. As it often did when reading, the time passed in the blink of an eye. I headed out into the main area to wait for the commander. He was already propped up in the corner waiting for me. The odd thing was, he was alone. A Lennox Corp Special Commander sitting unprotected in the middle of the slums; this was making me nervous. I calmly sat down eager to see what this was all about, and the commander, well, he got straight to it. He explained to me he feared he had a mole on the inside leaking details about his operations to people around the slums. It seems the thumb drive we had retrieved turned out to be a ghost drive. What he still wasn't sure of is if they meant to trick Lennox Corp or the intended buyer. The real point of our conversation was... he didn't care. He wanted Cloud 9 and the original thumb-drive.

This was where I came in, the Special Commander wanted to hire me to retrieve the drive from Cloud 9 and eliminate them permanently. He said, "I am close to knowing exactly where they are hiding". He continued, "When they unlock that drive, it will immediately begin broadcasting a signal to Lennox Corp letting us know the exact location". He then told me, "You cannot access a single Lennox Corp file, program or operating system without this feature immediately installing itself". He had said they were able to narrow Cloud 9's whereabouts down to 4 locations, and he wanted me to be ready to move when the signal broadcasted. The worst part was, he had teams at all 4 locations watching for any activity. One of the locations was the bunker. I couldn't go back there and risk being exposed. This meeting couldn't end fast enough. I had to warn J3 not to unlock that drive. The commander concluded our meeting by telling me I was the only one he had filled in because in his words "You're only in it for the credits. You couldn't care less what happens to these hackers." The only thing I could do was take the job. I'd need a plan to get us all out of this, before J3 finished unlocking that drive. All the planning and the danger to secure the thumb drive and the danger no one considered... the drive itself!

CHAPTER 8

Bunker Buster

I scrambled to figure out a way to contact J3 without being detected. The worst part, we still needed to open that drive even if I knew it would lead them straight to our location. The only way this would work was to wait for J3 to open the drive and let Lennox Corp pass the location on to me. I told the commander, once he gave me the location, I would move in quietly, take out Cloud 9 and then radio him. This would allow he and his men to move and gather whatever information they needed. He agreed to the plan, and I patiently waited for him to contact me with the location that I already knew. My only chance was to lure the commander and his men into the bunker and wipe out the whole team. This was an uncomfortable position to be in. An act like this would put me and Cloud 9 right to the top of the Lennox Corp's most wanted list. The fact remained, if the drive contained information that could bring down Lennox Corp, we owed it to the people to do everything in our power to hold on to that thumb drive.

I was getting very nervous at the thought of killing a Lennox Corp Special Commander. I had always maneuvered my way to stay off the Lennox Corp radar. Even though I felt reasonably confident in this operation, my second sight had a sense something was off. There are too many moving pieces all coming together at the same time for this not to be part of something much bigger that just hasn't revealed itself yet. After two uneventful days waiting around, I finally got the call from the Special Commander. They had located Cloud 9 in an old bunker but they weren't sure how to get inside. This was great news. I told the commander I knew the area and had scavenged the bunker several years earlier. I explained I should be able to find a way in. I suggested I go first and eliminate Cloud 9. Once I cleared the bunker, I would signal for the team to enter. This plan was acceptable to the commander, and he moved his team into position awaiting my call.

Making my way into the bunker, I saw J3 working feverishly, going through the data on the thumb drive. Surprised to see me, he said "Hey Tristan, we just unlocked the drive." I told him I didn't have time to explain but Lennox Corp was right outside the door. I urged him, "Copy off as much information as possible". J3 sorted through the files at blistering speed and suddenly there it was, the plans to a Lennox Corp barge, a list of security codes for shutting down an automated turret system, and the information just kept pouring out onto the screen. I couldn't believe what I was seeing. I had always thought the Lennox Corp barges were historic legends made more elusive as the rumors changed with each telling. This was no legend; I was seeing it all with my own eyes. There was a blueprint for a massive barge with automated security turrets and a staff of over 25 men and a technical staff of over 100. There was also a floor of the ship designated "Special Projects". The file for it was too deeply encrypted to open with the short time we had left. I decided we had seen enough for now. It was time to call the commander and his men down into the bunker so I could eliminate them; no witnesses, no survivors. If all went well, and I eliminated the Special Commander, we would have plenty of time to examine the contents of the drive. I sealed the thumb drive in a special case in my sack and radioed the Special Commander. I hoped we hadn't taken too long and raised the commander's suspicions.

As I opened the bunker door, a blinding flash

of light erupted, knocking me back into the bunker. As I came around, I heard a faint humming sound. While trying to regain my wits, I glanced up to see the bunker door being welded shut from the outside. When I looked behind me, I found the humming noise was four drones strategically placed in each of the corners. As the Cloud 9 team started coming to, I heard the Special Commander's voice come over a radio, "Mr. Tristan, great scavenger of the Wasteland, did you think you could outsmart me twice? I've been on to you since the first drive broke down and we lost Cloud 9. A man with a reputation like yours doesn't make mistakes he makes moves. This would have been your last chance to prove me wrong, but I decided why even worry about it, I will just bury all of you and the drive. The drones you see posted around you are the Lennox Corp Bunker Busters. I will detonate the drones at the end of this conversation burying everything and everyone. It is a shame. A man with your experience and knowledge of the Wasteland could have earned a lot of credits working with us. Instead, everything you own, all credits and all assets, now belong to Lennox Corp. "Take a deep breath; it will be your last!" The next few seconds felt like an eternity as the drones exploded. The poor kids from Cloud 9 were incinerated instantly. I had tried to find them and myself some cover, but I could feel the heat of the explosion as it seared my flesh off again and again as it kept trying to mend. Then, the bunker collapsed and the weight of the falling rubble began breaking bones. Finally, the rubble settled, but I was lying trapped underneath, struggling to breathe. The team was gone, the drive was most assuredly destroyed and I was fading fast. Just before blacking out, I remembered wondering if I would heal enough to claw my way out of this premature grave.

I laid there for days, in and out of consciousness. After 3 days, I began digging my way out a little at a time. The dust and ash kept filling my lungs making it very difficult for me to breathe or concentrate. I wasn't used to getting so tired, but I kept getting winded. Finally, after 3 more days of digging had passed, I could see daylight. I would wait for nightfall to reemerge into the world of the living. Everyone thought I was dead, and I needed to keep it that way for as long as possible. I lay under the last layer of rocks, staring through the cracks waiting for the sun to go down. Darkness finally came, and I somehow I pushed through the last layer of rock. Though I felt fatigued, being free was oddly invigorating. All I could think of now, find enough food and water to get myself right. It would take considerable strength to make the trip out to the bunker I called home.

There was no one anywhere around the site. Lennox Corp had closed it off and deemed it a crime scene. I was half naked and beat to shit, so I stayed near the shadows. I came across a tweaker passed out from a binge. I took his clothes and cautiously staggered my way through the slums grabbing and stealing food as I went. I found a quiet alley where I could eat and give my body more time to regenerate for the trip. It took about 30 minutes. I still needed a few supplies and a little more food and water. Another trip through the streets should do it. I grabbed all I could comfortably carry which consisted of mostly dumpster scraps and a gallon jug of dirty well water, but it would have to do. Now that I had enough supplies for the trip, I dragged myself out of the slums headed into the Wasteland. The food and water definitely helped, but I still felt off. I was experiencing dizzy spells and my breathing just wouldn't clear. I continued to cough up dust and ash. I needed to dig deep and make it home to my bunker. I had to recover and work on a new plan. Lennox Corp thought I was dead, and I planned to use that to my advantage. It took a couple more days of hiking than normal to reach my bunker. I kept having to stop or risk passing out. It thrilled me when I finally arrived at the hidden entrance. All I wanted to do was lock myself down somewhere and sleep. Things would present themselves with better clarity after I slept and the clean air should fix my breathing and stamina.

CHAPTER 9

Recovery

I Was so glad to be home I slept for the first 5 days only waking to drink water and grab a bite. I had stopped coughing up dust and ash, and, except for a dry wheezing feeling that remained in my lungs, I had recovered completely regaining full physical strength and energy. Mentally however, I was struggling to cope with the loss of J3 and Cloud 9. Taking down Lenox Corp was no longer my only priority. I would now add revenge on the commander to my list. After the bunker explosion, everyone would believe I was dead. Who could survive 4 simultaneous Bunker Buster explosions, right? The Special Commander was smart, fierce, and I will not underestimate him again. There could be no more mistakes. Taking out a high level member of the Lennox Corp security branch would stir up a shit storm for me no matter how I did it and at this point I really didn't care. Maybe it was time to stop hiding my gifts, though I was in no hurry to expose myself. Being assumed dead gave me a huge strategic advantage allowing me to continue my investigation into the Lennox Corp barge and room to devise a plan that would get me so close to the Special Commander, my eyes would be the last thing he saw as he took his final breath.

High-ranking members of Lennox Corp rarely left their assigned cities. It took very sensitive data being at risk to lure the commander into the slums. Those opportunities don't present themselves often. If I thought I could pull it off, I would try to get him from within the city. But to do that, not only would I need a way in, I would also need a way out. Even for me that sounded like a suicide mission. If I could stir up some trouble in the slums, by taking out a few of the Lennox Corp patrols, that might bring him out. It would prove difficult running an operation from inside my own slums, as everyone there knew me. Lennox Corp used the explosion and our deaths to further their propaganda campaign. To turn everyone against us, they falsely reported the confiscation of a biological weapon, built by Cloud 9, intended to spread a deadly virus in the slums. Though most see through the rhetoric, it was all the more reason to lie low. Seeing me alive would probably incite an uprising causing Lennox Corp to respond in such force I would never get a shot at the Special Commander, but an uprising was an intriguing thought. The deaths of several Lennox Corp officers wouldn't hurt my feelings, either. As I continued down this line of thinking, a plan began coming together. This would be a game of timing and precision and my involvement had to remain hidden. The element of surprise was my best friend. If the commander found out I was still alive, he would return to the safety of the city. To stir up a rebellion, I would need the help of my most trusted contacts in the slums. If we shake the tree hard enough, the fruit will fall.

My brain was telling me there was one other person I needed to see, but I wasn't trying to hear it. She lived in the deepest part of the marshland and I really didn't want to head out there after what I had just been through. Not to mention, the marshlands were home to the wild dog pack. My recent run in with the pack gave me a new appreciation of the power they possess. I had witnessed them in action, numbering well over 20 now. The Alpha looked bigger and stronger than ever. I recognized him from my childhood. He still wore the scar I had given him. He knew me as well; I could see it in his eyes as the pack gave chase. He had not forgotten our encounter. Knowing what I was heading into made me nervous about the trip. To make things worse, they had seized all my credits and assets leaving me on foot. I had plenty to trade, but I was dead so I had no way to take advantage of it. I knew where I would go next. My two main concerns now were avoiding others and avoiding that dog pack.

I had everything I needed now, just a 2 day hike to the marshlands and another 3 days into the central marsh and I was there. It is always easier said than done. I would sleep on it for a couple days and then make my way to the marshlands; this was not a trip to take lightly. The next 2 days were a twisted web of nightmares and half sleep. I just couldn't calm my mind down. I kept seeing Cloud 9 being incinerated by the explosion and it haunted me. I have seen a lot of death and experienced differing degrees of hell, and though I've contributed my share to both, these were just kids trying to do what they thought was right and the Special Commander dropped a bunker on their heads just because he could. As my rage grew, I couldn't wait any longer. I needed some answers before I set my sites on the commander. It was time to go see Claire.

I left out early the next morning, still dealing with a slight wheeze and a dry cough. I needed to push hard and make 30 miles each of the next 2 days to make the edge of the marsh and set up camp before I pushed inward through wild dog territory. Once I arrived at the marsh, I camped out a few days. I had come here to see Claire, but I had not spoken to or seen her for years. I really didn't even know what exactly to ask her or why I was so sure she could help. Part of me was hoping Claire could help me with this cough, but the main part figured she could offer insight into the information derived from the thumb drive.

Claire was once a top Lennox Corp tech scientist and doctor. She was banished many years ago after publicly releasing the cure for one of Lennox Corp's deadly viruses. She helped create the technological applications regarding citizenship entrance in and out of the city. It had been many years since she was a citizen and worked for Lennox Corp but many of the policies and applications she ushered in were still being used today. Nowadays, many residents of the slums referred to her as a witch believing she practiced the dark arts. Hell, it's been so long, there's a chance she won't remember me or worse, she is dead. I just had to hope she was still alive.

After two days camping at the edge of the marsh, I decided it was time to make the treacherous journey through the wild dog's territory to Claire's cabin. I got a few miles in before I became very uncomfortable. I could feel the pack watching my every move, just waiting for the perfect time to pounce. This was the second time recently that I felt true fear, and I was not a fan. Everything about the marsh was dangerous, and yet my only focus was on the dog pack. I set up camp a couple days in and built a massive fire to deter the Dog Pack, but I could still feel them watching me. I had finally fallen asleep when I suddenly startled awake with a nudge to my cheek. The Alpha was standing over me with a determined look in his eyes. He definitely knew me. They had been stalking me this entire time, waiting for me to get deep enough into the marsh that there was no escape. I lay there perfectly still; I wasn't sure how this would go down. The Alpha had blood and skin in his teeth, reeking of death and decay as he stood over me breathing heavily. I knew if I made a move, the pack would tear into me. The fear crept in but I had to act! I grabbed for the Alpha's throat and just as I expected the pack pounced. They were tearing into my flesh and gnawing at my bones. I could feel my body trying to keep up and repair itself, but the dogs were relentless, as the carnage continued. I felt myself getting dizzy; the panic was making my breathing issue flare up. It was too late; I could feel myself getting ready to pass out. Just as my eyes clamped closed, the dogs retreated in a panic. I forced them open for one last look. The dogs were retreating and the pain and lack of oxygen took its final toll as I passed out.

CHAPTER 10

Claire

I awoke, somewhat surprised, to find myself still alive. A bit confused, I looked around half expecting to find myself atop a pile of bones in the dog pack lair. Instead, I was in a comfortable bed with fresh linens. Next to me was a candle with the gentle aroma of incense and a fresh glass of water. I could hear the creaking of what sounding like a rocking chair gentle rolling over porch boards. I sat up, drank the water and pulled myself up out of the bed. I made my way to the doorway and there in the rocker sat Claire. She looked exactly as she had all those years ago. Claire looked around and said, "I heard you were dead." I asked her how she could have heard any-thing living way the hell out here. She responded, "I know, and I will always know everything that goes on in the cities, the slums and with you, Tris-tan." She urged, "So what brings you to me?" I had so many questions but I started with the ones that seemed the most significant at the moment. "First, how is it I'm not dead from the dog attack? I fully expected to wake up in the pack den if I sur-vived." She laughed, "That dog pack is con-trolled by Lennox Corp tech, they are all chipped with frequency adjusters that can drive and dic-tate their behavior. I hacked all of their chips years ago, and developed a jammer to inflict pain. Now they stay far away from here. Why do you think the dog pack never attacks Lennox Corp convoys and supply lines?" She then said, "You may not remember this, but Kalil brought you to me after the dog pack attacked you as a boy and I was the one that saved you. I was still working for Lennox Corp then. I snuck you both into the city, giving you a great gift. Not only did I save your life, but I gave you a taste of the cities lifeblood." I didn't understand. The look of confusion on my face must have been easier to read than a wanted poster. "Come sit down Tristan. I think it's time we talk." She began speaking again, and this time with even more purpose in her voice, "In an effort to save your life and heal your wounds, I injected you with Nano-technology. Nano-tech works by mixing with your blood stream and travels by RNA to embed itself in your DNA. It accentuates your strengths, presenting differently in each individual. One person may experience enhanced mental gifts; another may develop extraordinary physical strength. To what extent your gifts develop depends on your original potential." So, this is what they are hiding from the people of the slums. I could not believe what I was hearing. She continued, "Everyone who is a resident of the city receives an injection once early in their childhood and then again in their early 20s, allowing them to fulfill their ultimate potential. Those citizens of vital use to them, like your friend the Special Commander, receive regular injections to make sure they stay at the top of their game."

So, I wasn't special at all; I was just like all the residents of the city.   Or was that the case? She has kept track of me all this time for a reason, and I was feeling uneasy to learn what reason that may be. I had to ask, "Why am I so important to you? Am I your special project?" At this point my anger was speaking. Her response only added to my tensions. She calmly responded, "No, you are the Savior." She explained that after she saved me, she tried to expose Lennox Corp and give everyone control, not only to the cure of the virus, but to Nano-tech. Lennox Corp banned her from all cities and slums condemning her to a life in the Wasteland. She kept track of me and was in touch with Kalil regularly because she had seen no one react the way I did to Nano-tech. My body almost instantly healed all of my injuries and infused with the Nano-tech making me one with the technology. She said I was Nano-tech and Nano-tech was me. I told her my healing properties had developed to the point I was almost impossible to kill. I have always wondered about my tactical awareness, advanced ability to process information and capacity for comprehension in learning; these skills were all gifts of Nano-tech. This too explains my need to read books. She then said, "I believe you can only improve with more injections and I could help you with that, but I want you to think about it first. Today has revealed much and you, I'm sure, are tired from the attack." I didn't know about all this Savior stuff she was preaching, but I will do whatever it takes to get to the Special Commander. I headed back in to rest feeling like I had created more questions than answers.

It surprised me how well I had rested considering all I had on my mind. I had thought about it a lot before I fell off to sleep last night; I definitely wanted the next injections.   Once again, I heard the lonely creaking of the rocking chair on the front porch. I walked out on the porch to see Claire gently moving back and forth. I asked, "Do you sleep?" She answered, "Not much, one of my side effects from the Nano-tech is I don't sleep but 2 or 3 hours a week. As you have probably noticed, I also don't age at a normal rate." As we enjoyed a cup of coffee together, I told her I was ready for the next injections. We enjoyed the sounds of the marsh coming alive while we had some breakfast. And as we finished up, we decided now was as good a time as any.

While she was giving me the injections, I was already starting to see that I had spent all of my years scavenging and learning the Wasteland just so I could pretend that Lennox Corp wasn't oppressing everyone. I told myself that was my life, but really I was just refusing to see reality. Within minutes I could feel the Nano-tech working in my body, in my mind. I felt heightened levels of thoughts, ideas and dreams. I also developed more questions like, what made Kalil bring me to her in the first place. I looked at Claire and said, "Why did Kalil, bring me to you?" She smiled and responded. "Let the Nano-tech do its job and then search your thoughts and you tell me the answer." I sat there piecing together all the possible connections and then, as if I were looking at a board with the answers on it, the truth appeared, "Are You My Mother?" I said surprising even myself. Softly, a smile graced her face, and she responded, "Yes Tristan, I am."

Claire explained, "Childbirth is one freedom you give up to be a citizen. I truly believed that the only way I could help everyone was from the inside, so I hid my pregnancy and gave birth in the slums leaving you in the care of Kalil. I immediately asked who my father was. She replied that she had artificially inseminated herself to create a child that would be extra responsive to Nanotech hoping he would one day grow up to save the people and now here I stood, the Savior." This was all beginning to sound overwhelming yet it was making sense. Maybe I have a responsibility here, a higher calling to help the people. It made sense now why it was never enough, I was always looking for the next adventure. She had been plotting behind the scenes for years waiting for the right time to reveal herself to me and to take down Lennox Corp and now I came to her with an agenda of my own to take down Lennox Corp.

Things were taking an eerie shape. As I tried wrapping my head around the fact that Claire was my mother, it only exacerbated the issues I was having understanding myself. I felt like I needed some time to process it all and headed back to the bedroom for a nap. I still needed sleep. When I awoke this time, I was feeling much better. She asked me if I was experiencing any new effects from the Nano-tech and I immediately noticed that my breathing issues had disappeared. So much had happened; I had completely forgotten I was having trouble. I also noticed I had no soreness or residual pain from the dog attack. My memory recall was seeing every detail of every situation as I recalled them like a catalogue in my mind. So as soon as I thought about the Barge, the information from the thumb drive appeared in my mind just as it had on the computer screen in the bunker. I now truly understood why it was so easy for the Special Commander to figure me out and outsmart me. The feeling was crazy! I had always had them in me but I could feel them working now on every level of my being, not just as a physical trauma repair process.

As more information came to me, I asked my mother if she had ever heard of the Barge. Claire began to explain, "The Barge is the lifeline of all three cities. The servers necessary to run the cities and control the citizen's reside on the Barge. No one really knows the specifics of the Barge, but be sure the Barge does exist." My focus shifted to the Special Commander. He still took the top spot on my list. Lennox Corp could wait. My mother had already dug up all the information that she could on the Special Commander and current Lennox Corp security protocols. It turned out that even before my latest injections I was on to something. If we could get the slums to revolt against Lennox Corp, that would bring out the Special Commander. I will still need a way to get close to him. Between my resources and Claire's resources, we had a real chance to stir up enough shit to get a real rise out of Lennox Corp. Her plan started with capturing the dog pack and manipulating their signal to attack Lennox Corp supply lines. That should force them to cut back aid to the slums creating tension. Planting the seeds of revolt around the slums would be stage 2. That would be topped off by hanging a few Lennox Corp patrols in the public square with anti-Lennox Corp propaganda poster pinned to their chest. That should trigger a level 3 warning which will bring out the big hitters and a curfew for the slums. This should be the chaos necessary to bring on the wrath of the Special Commander himself. Once we get him out into the slums, I will reveal myself and kill him for all to see setting off a riot and uprising like Lennox Corp has never seen. When the people see his men firing on me and I continue to take them out, healing every step of the way, the people will hopefully rise up with me to take down Lennox Corp. There was a lot to process and even more to do. Many questions remained for my mother.

CHAPTER 11

New Alpha

My mother and I parted ways as she went to the slums to gather a network that could help us with the uprising. I had always been an above average strategist, but I could now feel the Nano-tech working overtime. I was formulating solutions at a remarkable pace, and each was more efficient than the one before. The most amazing part, none of the plans involved me getting shot or blown up. Most had a high probability of sustaining no injuries and I could see all of them like process diagrams in my head. The plan to focus on now, leading the dog pack into an ambush. There was an area of the marsh that once was a lake and the sludge has a special consistency that encompasses anything that decides to cross. If I used my mother's swamp buggy to lure them in, they would become stuck and ultimately succumb to the pull of the muck. The lowlands are usually shallow but should be deep enough the buggy will sink. I would require a way out.

I transported all of Claire's firewood down to the old lake, behind her buggy. I would fasten the timber together, constructing a bridge, and force it out into the middle of the bog. I used a roll of Lennox Corp manufacturing wire to join the logs. Claire had an entire spool of the stuff. When I completed the bridge, the density and size should allow it to rest on top of the mud. This should make a solid structure to pull myself out, but be short enough; the pack would never reach it. I then fastened the wire around the trunks of two trees for security. The work went quick. I can't count the nights I would lie awake thinking about trekking into the marsh, locating their lair and burning them out. I would fantasize about it coming down to just me and the alpha. I will experience such freedom when I am standing over the alpha's corpse. I honestly never built up the courage to act against them. I've known they couldn't kill me, but they were unquestionably capable of inflicting severe trauma physically and mentally. This time things seemed different, I wasn't attacking them; I was removing them. The satisfaction I would experience was real, yes, but I was seeing the bigger picture of how the removal of the dog pack would benefit trade and commerce between the slums and remove another Lennox Corp tool. Let's hope Claire sees it the same way. Advanced Nano-tech or not, my heightened level of understanding was dealing with this issue the same as it had in the past; destroy them.

After I finished building my lifeline out of the mud, I chilled for a while and tried to digest everything I had learned in the last few days.

The pack's territory spread out over 100 acres and I could drive around in the buggy for days and never see them. I was better off letting them come to me. I kept mulling over the information I had gathered so far. Lennox Corp was running the slums of S.C. 1 as an off-the-books project. I had not been to the slums of S.C. 2, but according to Captain Chip it appeared to be run by Lennox Corp as well. I didn't really understand what Chip meant because, whose books were we talking about? Lennox Corp always ran the show and certainly never cared much about what went on in the slums. Their interest in controlling the slums seemed nominal. They take what they want from us and provide little in return. The Special Commander left the safety of the city just to hire me. He could have sent any one of their professionals to retrieve the Lennox Corp property. Not to mention, if once opened the thumb drive revealed the location, why did they need help at all. This puzzle presented me with more pieces and fewer spaces to put them in. Knowing that I had been being played by the Special Commander, I couldn't help but wonder if this was about the drive at all. I felt like the Special Commander had his own agenda and had singled me out through some evaluation process. I just couldn't see why or how I even ended up on the Lennox Corp radar, but something definitely didn't add up. I knew Claire's plans involved the destruction of Lennox Corp and I was on board. But I also had to take care of the Special Commander. Sometimes I question whether Lennox Corp are the ones in control anymore. Dealing with this new train of thought proved dizzying; I didn't know yet how to turn it off. There was a maze of possibilities coming at me constantly. I read a book once that taught you how to calm your mind with meditation and if ever there was a time to meditate, this was it. Hopefully I could follow it with some sleep.

Meditation usually proves to be soothing

and I could feel myself drifting into the quiet of my sub-conscience. Sleep followed, but in a few hours I awoke with a slight stinging sensation all over my body. To my utter disgust, I was covered in marsh leeches. I hate marsh leeches. Their prong teeth made them a nightmare to remove, and the venom numbs your skin for hours. After an hour of painstaking removal, I moved quickly to set myself up a proper camp in which to wait for the pack. While I worked, I was developing an alternate plan to bring about the demise of the Special Commander. Everyone thought I was dead including the Special Commander. Instead of trying to lure him out to the slums, this could be my chance to sneak in to the city. He was playing the game at a different level and would always be ready for any attack that I launched on him outside of the city. But inside, where he felt safe and secure, I could catch him with his guard down. The more I dwelled on an uprising, the more uncomfortable I became with the dangers of starting a revolution. I was still carrying the guilt of the deaths of the kids from Cloud 9. There were people I cared about in the slums; I could not bear a massacre. An excuse to initiate a lockdown and assert their authority could be exactly what Lennox Corp was looking for to gain control of our slums, just like the others. Captain Chip had mentioned that both slums had fallen deeper into crime and violence right before Lennox Corp took them over. I started thinking about the rise in crime in my own slums and the new low life's trying to take advantage of the struggling people. There was a high probability that Lennox Corp had orchestrated this downfall and were now preparing S.C. 3 for the same fate as S.C.1 and S.C.2. It looks like I will need to contact Claire to get me into the city. After I remove the dog pack, I will return to the slums and put together a plan to sneak inside the city and kill the Special Commander. We could proceed with the plot to take down Lennox Corp once the Special Commander was out of the picture. I owed it to Cloud 9 to crush the Special Commander's skull with my bare hands. First things first, the dog pack had to go. I decided my time of reflection was passed. I had arrived at the time of action.

As the evening approached, I reached in my bag and pulled out my bow and arrows. It was time to hunt. If I killed two wild pigs, their blood would make a great perimeter marker to lure the dog pack to my part of the marsh, speeding up this waiting game. The wild pigs ran in packs and were mean as hell, but not very smart. You usually find them feeding wherever there were marsh frogs. A marsh frog hotbed was located not far from the camp. I waited until well after midnight and made my way to the site. I was not disappointed. I spotted multiple wild pigs, scouting out the smorgasbord. I watched their activity for a few minutes, picking out the two fattest pigs. The fatter the pig the shorter the run and I was in no mood for a late night run through the marsh. I silently crept in behind them hitting the pigs with perfectly placed arrows to the neck. The impact sent both panicked hogs sprinting off in different directions. One pig made it about 80 ft while the other barely sprinted out 30 ft before falling over. I had chosen my pigs wisely. They weighed over 300 pounds each so I hiked back for the swamp buggy and dragged them down to the campsite. I set up a few pails under the carcasses while I skinned and gutted the pigs packing up some of the more edible meat for later. I took the blood that I drained in the pails and spread it all around about 150 yards outside of camp. That amount of blood should catch the attention of the pack if they are anywhere within 30 miles of my camp. Hopefully, they would be the only predators attracted to the camp. I made a small fire and cooked up some of my pig meat and waited patiently.

On warm nights like this, the lights in the

sky are particularly strange. Tonight proved especially active, and I found myself mesmerized until
that feeling of someone watching crept over me
once again. The pack was near I could sense them.
I was very familiar with this sensation, and I was
usually right. Since the attack when I was a boy, I
have had a strange connection to the dog pack and
they to me. This pack may be ruthless and dom-
inate the Wasteland, but they are very cautious of
me. They were creeping closer and closer; the hair
on my neck was standing straight out. It was time
to get this party started, so I crawled over to the
buggy, jumped in and cranked it up with a loud
rumble of the engine. As the floodlights lit, I could
see their eyes reflecting in the night. I sped off,
heading away from the lake. As they came out of
cover, I saw the alpha sprinting out with a determined expression on his face, the rest of the pack
following his every move. I led them on a chase
through the marsh. My best bet for success was
to exhaust them. When I could tell they were fad-

ing, I headed back down to the old lake. I drove straight toward the lake gaining speed the entire way. I looked behind me and noticed the alpha pulling back as the rest of the pack continued to give chase. Thankfully, the dogs followed me right into the mud. The bog was unrelenting and the more they fought to get to me, the stronger the mud pulled them back and eventually down to their muddy grave. The alpha had not followed. The buggy was sinking prematurely, just short of my lifeline. I gunned it, forcing it further into the middle of the lake. Grasping onto the bridge I worked myself towards the shore. Pulling myself to freedom, I immediately gathered up my things, starting with the frequency jammer for the dog's chips. The Alpha was still not around, but I wasn't taking any chances. The jammer may be my only hope against him. I got my backpack together, smothered my fire and started the walk back to Claire's cottage. After a long hike through the night, I could finally see the glow from the lights at the cottage. I was only a few miles out now.

Out of nowhere, I took a sudden hard blow to the side. The alpha had been stalking me and made his move. Jammer still in hand, I pressed the button as he lunged for my throat. He tried to fight it, but began howling and thrashing with pain. I pulled out my long knife, but before striking the killing blow, the alpha passed out from the pain. I turned the jammer off, and for a reason unbeknownst to me, I found I couldn't kill him. I muzzled him using an old rag in my bag. I decided to carry him back with me. Once I got him back to the cottage, I went through Claire's meds and found something to knock him out. I needed to remove the Lennox Corp chip. Without it in, I could determine his true nature. I locked him in an outbuilding with a bowl of pig meat and some water. I would monitor him for now. If he attacked when he came around, It would make my decision on what to do with him very easy. For now, my plan was to release him into the wild.

While the alpha was out, I decided it was a good time for me to get some rest, too. I had only been asleep for a short time, when I was yanked awake by his howling and giving the door to the outbuilding a pounding. While sitting on the edge of the bed, I remembered having the craziest dream where I talked to the alpha dog and he and I came to an understanding. Man, this Nanotech was really doing a number on me. Even my dreams were expressing a higher level of crazy. It was time to let him out and observe his behavior. I was hoping he would just run off and go back to his life in the wild, though his pack now rested at the bottom of the muddy lake. The truth be told, he would be far less dangerous alone. I approached the outbuilding and slowly opened the door. He came out with a furious rage, spun around to me snarling and growling, but he didn't attack. As soon as he got his bearings, we made eye contact. As I stood unwavering, staring straight back into his eyes, his demeanor changed. His tail went down and the hair on his back receded. He put his head down in submission and approached me with respect. The alpha knew he had been defeated, and now I was the pack leader.

I took the next couple days preparing for my trip back to the slums. The alpha was healing quickly from the chip removal and he never left my side. We seemed fated to be together in this adventure. As homage to my friend the blacksmith, I named the alpha Smith. I felt a sense of comfort with Smith around; he kept watch and protected me. His pack had been strong for a reason, and now we were a pack. I couldn't believe the same dog that haunted my dreams for so many years would now protect me in my life. I guess the Wasteland had a new alpha, and I was assembling my pack.

CHAPTER 12

A Way Inside

I have not cut my hair or shaved my beard since the collapse of the bunker. This was a tactical decision, as I knew the time would come when I would return to the slums and I didn't want to be easily recognized. Smith would offer another form of cover as most people shy away from the wild dogs. Smith and I made our way through the Wasteland on foot as every mode of transportation was blown up, wrecked or sunk. Telling my mother about the swamp buggy would not be fun, especially having used it to eliminate the dog pack. Claire should be at Tammy's. I suggested she stay there once she arrived in the slums. We would need Tammy's help at some point and she had always been loyal to me. I also wanted Claire to tell Tammy I was still alive. Tammy is one of only a handful of people that would be personally affected by my death.

Smith made a great traveling companion, and we arrived back at the slums after only a few days. Just as I expected, no one seemed to recognize me and Smith made sure people kept their distance. I walked on to Tammy's, and she was not fooled by my new look, but played along and directed me to wait in Claire's room. My mother was out, most assuredly making contact with her people on the inside. I still wasn't sure if I fully trusted Claire or her motivations, but she was my mother and I wanted to give her the benefit of the doubt. Smith and I rested in her room while we waited for her to show up. Within a few hours, she arrived and expressed her displeasure to see me with my new friend Smith. She screamed "I told you to turn that monster against its creator not adopt him!" I explained the dog pack posed an ongoing threat, so I removed them from the equation instead of turning them on Lennox Corp. I described leading the pack into the mud lake, using her swamp buggy. "My swamp buggy?" she said. I said my apologies, and quickly moved on to how Smith and I came to be companions. Although she did not exactly agree with my choices, especially the part where I confiscated and sank her buggy, she somewhat reluctantly accepted my decision. Smith however was not a fan of Claire, and I had to correct him multiple times for growling at her. Maybe he remembered her using the jamming device on him and the dog pack. Time would tell. All in all, Smith's willingness to serve me and his overall impressive intelligence continued to trump his animal instincts. I couldn't have been more pleased. I had my concerns, bringing him around so many people, but it really was that damn Lennox Corp microchip making him crazy. The connection I had with him was so powerful that it honestly felt like all I had to do was visualize a command and he would interpret it.

I was just about to tell Claire about my latest scheme to capture the Special Commander when suddenly she spoke up, "I have a new plan. I think you should capture the Special Commander inside the city and I can help you do it." I couldn't believe what I was hearing, and then it hit me. If she was my mother and was actively injecting herself with Nano-tech, then the obvious conclusion would be that our DNA and the close match in intelligence would lead us to the same strategic solution. Instead of working on a way to start a riot she had already been greasing the wheels and setting up the connections to get me inside of S.C. 3. She still had connections on the inside and knew which Lennox Corp security agents she could pay to look the other way. They, of course, mustn't know it was me they were helping. There should be an opportunity to sneak me inside in the next few days. In the meantime I needed to stay out of sight. I couldn't risk being recognized.

I had one errand of my own to take care of, I wanted to see Laura and let her know that I was alive. The next morning, before most of the slums were up I headed over to the blacksmith shop. Laura was genuinely shocked and pleased to see me. She told me that the inhabitants of the slums had tried to have a memorial service for me and the members of Cloud 9. The Special Commander himself showed up and shut the entire service down. He gave a speech where he announced to everyone in the slums that things would soon be changing. There seemed to be some question as whether he believed I was deceased, and he was offering a huge reward to anyone who delivered my dead body to him. This statement definitely sparked my curiosity. Why would he even consider the notion I was still alive? I described a small, sharp knife I had been thinking about, to

Laura. I needed it to be small enough to smuggle into the city. Laura listened as I gave her further details and then she told me to come back tomorrow and she would have my knife ready. She reached down and stroked Smith on the head. "So who's your new friend?" she said. I told her he was a stray I had picked up. My heart swelled a bit as I watched how he instantly warmed up to her. This only confirmed how I already felt about her since the first time we met. She then said, "He's seems like a nice guy. Let me know if you ever need somebody to watch him." I thanked her for the offer. I would need somebody I could trust to watch him while I was in the city, and Laura was the first person he had liked since I brought him to the slums. Smith and I returned to Tammy's after I talked with Laura. I decided we would just hangout the rest of the day. The more I was out and about the higher the risk of being seen.

Claire came in looking like it had been quite

a long day. We went over what was accomplished so far but she said she still had a few loose ends to tie up to assure my safe passage into the city. I thanked her for everything. Things were moving so fast, I really hadn't had a chance to do that yet. She smiled, took my hand and said, "We both know what we have to do". After she left, I reflected back to the Special Commander's statement. Might he be aware of my abilities, maybe even from the beginning? What else did he know? What was he really after with me? Those were a few of the questions forming in my mind. When Claire returned later that evening, she came and found me to finalize the details and solidify the plan. "Before we move on, would you mind answering a few more questions concerning the Nano-tech technology?" I said. Her eyes met my gaze and remained steady as she spoke, "I know this is important to you and I'm always ready to answer your questions".

I wanted to understand Nano-tech better, but more importantly, I needed to learn the vulnerabilities. Claire decided it was best to start from the beginning and I agreed. Apparently she was among the first to develop Nano-tech and began injecting herself early in the process to prevent Lennox Corp from testing it on unknowing members of the slums. She explained to me, back then only S.C. 1 existed and that Lennox Corp was not the only Corporation operating in the world. This was very confusing, mind you; all I had ever known was Lennox Corp, the cities, the slums and the Wasteland. My mother said this was the way Lennox Corp wanted it. They couldn't risk losing resources and workers to other Corporations, as Lennox Corp was already the smallest and weakest of the remaining corporations. Apparently, there were two other Corporations operating beyond the Wasteland, Bliskin Corp. and Clarity Corp. Bliskin Corp was the big dog and a percentage of everything Lennox Corp and Clarity Corp produced went to Bliskin Corp for the right to operate. The next part really blew my mind. My mother had been part of the team responsible for the creation of Nano-tech. A few team members opted to inject themselves, which allowed the technology to advance at a rapid pace. In only a few short years, the team had Nano-tech targeting specific traits of a person, making them faster, stronger and smarter; but Lennox Corp's favorite was smarter. After the advance of Nano-tech, Lennox Corp put a plan into motion to overthrow the other two corporations and take control. They began testing everyone, even the people in the slums, looking for people with above average intelligence. They then took these people away. No one ever saw them again. In the meantime, the residents of the slums believed they had given the people a better life as a member of the city. What she said next turned my stomach, "In reality, they were being taken to the Barge and placed into medically induced comas, pumped full of Nano-tech and hooked up to massive computer systems." I could now see the entire picture. "So, there are no servers; the people are the servers", I said. My mother seemed pleased with my ability to understand the direction of this tragic story. She said to me with deep concern in her eyes, "You see now why I went into hiding? The only way to stop Lennox Corp is to take out that barge and kill thousands of innocent, unknowing people." I could now see the moral dilemma she had dealt with her entire life. She said, "Now is the time to fight back. Lennox Corp is strengthening their forces and taking over the slums trying to drafting unwilling residents into combat to fight against the other corporations. They had all the brain power they needed; they have produced plenty of weapons, now they just needed an army. We have to stop them." There was still much more I wanted to know, but I knew we needed to move on to the plan we had formulated. Claire said the pieces were set in play quicker than expected and I was good to enter the city tomorrow night.

Lennox Corp had become arrogant, believing their cities to be impenetrable, but years of mistreatment to the city's people had led to corruption against Lennox Corp. My mother had an entire network of workers on the inside that would be at my disposal if I needed them. I hoped to accomplish the task alone and be back in the slums before anybody knew what happened. It was nice to know that I had a support system within the city if things got complicated. The deeper in I went, the more it became about getting answers than revenge. I needed to take my time with the Special Commander and persuade him to talk. If Claire and I were going to take down Lennox Corp, the Special Commander could prove vital to our success.

CHAPTER 13

The City

Claire and I developed a solid scheme for getting into the city. If everything flowed to plan, that part should be easy. Unfortunately, the only sure way to get out of the city without being detected is the waste outflow tunnel. Though not a glamorous escape, it gives me the best opportunity to escape the city undetected. Claire would make sure I had a vehicle available on the other side of the outflow. The more I reviewed the logistics, the more I realized I would never have the time I needed to interrogate the Special Commander while we were in the city. I needed to incapacitate him and drag him through the outflow tunnel with me. I had to get

him back to my bunker where I could break him.
We need his intel to dismantle Lennox Corp.

Getting me into the city worked just as
planned. My mother's people created a small distraction near the guard tower of the East entrance.
She paid the two men manning the post to inspect
the disturbance without calling it in to the central security and they earned their credits. Claire
had bribed the guards at the gate to look the other
way while her friend escorted me through the
checkpoint. Once we were past the checkpoint, he
took me back to his lab and updated my microchip with security code giving me access around
the city. He gave me a keycard and an address to a
house where I could stay stocked with food, cloth-
ing and a vehicle to use while in the city. When I
went to thank him, he rushed me to a door at the
other end of the basement and said "good luck". It
seems the interaction among citizens is limited to
work relationships, any interactions beyond that

are discouraged, so this rush was not surprising. I laid low for the evening in my new house. Hopefully, the downloaded security code will allow me access to the places I need to go while shadowing the commander. My goal was to find the weakness in his routine so I could isolate and remove him without being detected. I hoped to be back at the bunker deep in discussion with the commander before anyone even knew he was missing.

Claire's contact Clarence had provided me with the Special Commander's domicile location and that was where I planned to start. I arrived very early and took up a covert position. The Special Commander would never expect me to be here shadowing him, but he was highly intelligent and not to be underestimated. Once he left the house, I stayed quite a distance behind him but close enough to avoid losing him, using the crowded streets as cover. The first couple of days, trailing him through the city, I couldn't help but notice that much of what we had been told about the city was a lie. I had heard about the interaction rules, but the atmosphere was one of a cold, dead city run by artificial intelligence. It felt like a tragic cultural sterilization had taken place. There was no interaction outside of work. Everywhere I looked, the mindless faces passed right by me, never even looking me in the eyes; work, home repeat. This society had relinquished the freedom of the true emotions that come with living like joy, anger, love, and hate to satisfy their superficial desires of physical perfection and monetary fulfillment. I always thought the Lennox Corp had enslaved the slums, but the reality is they have enslaved the cities and now they want the slums, my slums. I had seen all that I needed to see these last couple of days. I must shut Lennox Corp down for good.

I spent 3 days following the Special Commander. He was a very particular man. Every day he ate breakfast at 7:30 a.m. in his Sun Room with the skylight open, followed by a rigorous 1hr. workout routine. He then closes the skylight and heads to the shower. Exactly 35 minutes after his workout his security convoy shows up and they begin their rounds. All day long he goes from branch to branch of the Lennox Corp security tree monitoring production and checking for ineffi-ciencies and security protocol breeches. He never skips a branch. The day takes about 12 hours and has a sinister grind to it. I never saw him eat lunch. So far, I have not seen an opportunity present it-self during the day. He is surrounded by security whether in a car, on the sidewalk or walking the halls of the security branches. After he completes the review of the last branch, his security con-voy drops him off at home. Here, he heads out to his sunroom, opens the skylight and stares at the sky while he eats his dinner. He takes in another protein paste about 30 minutes after dinner, and grinds out another 1hr workout. After completing the workout, he enjoys one last gaze through the skylight, about 10 minutes worth, and then shuts it down to head for the showers and bed. I will have to hit him at home. Anywhere else would be suicide even for me. I just had to bide my time and wait for him to make a mistake.

I stopped following him to work and instead focused my energies on surveillance of the home and how he spent his time there. I began watching him every second he was home, waiting for my opportunity. I believed I had found a way to get to him, but I still had to get inside the house. In the meantime, I had Clarence pick up a few things I thought I would need. A few adjustments to his biometric security panel should give him a jolt, but less than 30,000 volts. I want him incapacitated not dead; not yet. I could then inject him with a tranquilizer. Hopefully, he won't wake until we are through the outflow pipe. I spent almost 2 weeks watching him go through the same routine every morning and every night. His routine was unrelentingly diligent. I was thinking I would have to go kamikaze if I didn't get in soon.

Finally, the break I had been waiting for was here. He received a call and cut his workout short. He had headed to the shower without shutting the skylight. I watched as the security team arrived and he headed to the front door. I anxiously waited for him to leave. He glanced back at the skylight, as if talking himself into leaving it open, and headed on out for his daily rounds. I knew he would be gone 12 hours, and I only needed 20 minutes. I scaled up the side of the house onto the roof and dropped down through the open sky-light. I immediately headed for the biometric panel and got to work. The tech was good, but out-dated. You could tell they had grown comfortable in their security and lived without fear of attack, at least from outside the walls of the city. It only took me 15 minutes to wire the panel. Now it was a waiting game. After what felt like a very long day of anticipation I could hear the convoy rumbling up the street right on time. I tucked back into my cranny and prepared the tranquilizer as the Special Commander approached the door. Just like I had planned it, zap, and it knocked the Special Commander back on his ass. I could tell he was only dazed, so I moved quickly. I pushed hard on his flank, sinking the needle into his neck and putting him to sleep. I dragged his body inside, tied his hands up and wrapped him in a sheet. I cleaned up the area and carried him outside, throwing his body into the trunk. Through back roads and alley ways, I made my way to the outflow pipe. There was a curfew, so a citizen spotting me was of no concern, but if a patrol spotted us it was game over. I parked the vehicle as close as possible but the walk to the outflow pipe was still half a mile away. I stayed in the darkest areas I could find stopping every few meters to check my surroundings and put the Special Commander down. I could see the outflow tunnel but there were patrols in the area and no way to reach them right now. I stashed the commander's body and watched to determine how many patrols I was facing. There were three 2 man patrols one of them was stationary guarding the Waste outflow pipe. It was clear they knew this was a weak point, and kept a presence around it at all times. I began clocking the patrols timing their rounds, and found a window for attack. The patrol on the outskirts had a 3 minute window where they were not visible to either of the other patrols. I focused on them first. I wanted to keep it quiet, so swift and silent with my bare hands would be the weapon of choice. I made my way to the blind spot. There was a small outbuilding with old generators in it. I'm guessing it was an old workshop. I climbed on top to take a position. As they approached, I waited for them to pass under me, and leaping from the building I knocked both men down to the ground. I pinned one man with my knee grabbing the other man around the neck as I fell. I choked the life from the man in my arms then applied added pressure from my knee crushing the second man's windpipe. The life fluttered from his eyes. I removed the men's knives and made my way up to where the second patrol was working. I snuck right past them and took out the two guarding the pipe, dumping them down the chute. Just as I had expected the remaining patrol was making their rounds, no idea the other patrols around them were dead. I had no time to play with these two. I got within range and hit both of them in the back with the cold steel of the knives. I dragged the rest of the bodies over and dumped them into the waste outflow pipe. I needed to cover my tracks for as long as possible.

Having cleared the way to the outflow chute, I returned to the Special Commander to find him still sleeping like a baby. I threw him over my shoulders and headed for the pipe. I took a deep breath and prepared myself mentally for what I was about to do. I dropped the Special Commander down the pipe first. I was right behind him following his sliding body through the waste outflow. This ride was not for the faint of heart, surrounded by trash and feces while being thrown around an old rusty pipe. This was not my idea of a good time. After what felt like an eternity we came spitting out into the Wasteland on top of a monster pile of waste and debris that had to have been collecting since the beginning of Lennox Corp. I fished the Special Commander's body out of the sloppy mess and once again threw him over my shoulders. As planned, Claire managed to have a vehicle waiting for me. We had made it out of the city and now were only a few miles away from my bunker. I would have the Special Commander singing in no time. I turned my focus to the task at hand, but as I looked back, I couldn't help but reflect on the truths revealed about the city.

CHAPTER 14

Interrogation

After what seemed like an extremely long ride, with the stench of the outflow permeating everything, I needed a shower desperately, not to mention a little sleep. The commander would be a better candidate for interrogation if I saved his shower for later, plus I wasn't ready to bring him around. He would wake up soon and probably in a panic. I didn't need him waking me. Besides, I always prefer to interrogate a person when I am fresh, giving me a mental and physical position of power. I slept like a baby knowing that the Special Commander was locked up tight and in my possession. I woke up the next morning and as I passed him, I could see the fear in his eyes. I took my time getting to him. I took a stroll around the yard to stretch my legs. I made myself some breakfast and then sat over in the corner to read for a little while. After a few hours, I approached the Special Commander, strung him up by his under arms in a very uncomfortable position and removed his gag. He didn't say a word he was waiting to see what approach I intended to use. I explained to him that this would go one of two ways: I ask the questions and he answers on his own or I ask the questions and force him to answer. The choice was his to make. I gave him some water and then put his gag back in. I then picked up my book and returned to reading. The psychological warfare would break him not the physical so I wanted to assert myself mentally right away and let him think about his choices. We both knew this wouldn't end well but only I knew exactly how it would end. Once I had the information needed to take down Lennox Corp, I would crush his skull.

The time had come to see which path the commander had chosen. I removed the gag and asked the commander "How long were you on to me?" He responded arrogantly "Not too long after I hired you for the first job." My next question was an easy one "How did you know about me?" He chuckled and answered "When you do a job you best finish it. You took out Waylon's Serpents, who worked for me by the way, but you didn't get Waylon did you? Waylon watched from a lookout tower as you proceeded to take out his entire crew. In disbelief, he of course headed straight to me." I then asked the commander, "How did you know I was still alive after the Bunker Busters exploded?" He smirked, "I didn't. I was just being cautious after the story Waylon told me. I knew you weren't special just enhanced by Nano-tech. The thing I don't know is how." "We will get to that. I'm asking the questions and you are answering them remember?" I said reminding him who was running this show. This man was no stranger to the techniques of interrogation. I continued with my next question, "What is the barge and how do I find it?" He began laughing; I didn't take him for the type who ever laughed. He responded, "Is that what this is about? You think you can take down Lennox Corp. Do you know what the barge is?" he said. I came back sharply, "Yes I do. It's where they stock a ship with innocent people pumped full of Nano-tech and use their brains as servers to run Lennox Corp." The look of shock on his face was priceless, I had him. I told him I also knew about the other corporations and the plan Lennox Corp had to overthrow them and rise to power. You could tell he was feeling defeated his entire demeanor changed. I asked him again, reminding him of the questioning rules. "Where is the barge and how do I access it?" "I can't tell you that and you know I can't." He muttered. I fixed my hand into a firm pointed arrow and dug my fingers in between his ribs, moving them back and forth in the ribcage. He screamed out in excruciating pain. I looked him deep in the eyes as I whispered, "This will get much worse before it gets better. You will beg me to kill you. Answer the question and save yourself the pain and me the pleasure." You could see that he was already starting to crack; he wasn't used to being on the receiving end. It was time to solidify my position and speed up the process. I reached over with a pair of wire cutters and removed his left thumb. As he screamed, I took my small torch and cauterized the wound; the commander passed out. I sat patiently waiting for him to come out of it. After a few minutes, the pain brought him around. As he regained focus on me, I held the torch up where he could see it. I asked him, "Would you like me to talk for a few minutes while you get the details about the barge in order?" I could tell he still needed a little more time. I went on, "You wanted to know how I ended up with Nano-tech inside of me? Well Special Commander, I am Nano-tech!"

You could see the commander's mind doing circles, between the pain and the information, he was overloading. He wasn't used to feeling weak, unable to control his situation or his fate. He had always been the one in control and he thought he knew every threat to Lennox Corp, yet, here I was growing up right under the proverbial nose of Lennox Corp and him. It pained him greatly to speak, but you could tell he needed to know so he asked. "What do you mean you are Nano-tech?" It was my turn to laugh. I responded, "I'm starting to realize your information has limitations, Special Commander." So I filled him in, observing his confusion and disbelief. "My mother was one of the original scientists that invented Nano-tech. When she learned how Lennox Corp was using it, she artificially inseminated herself with an embryo and Nano-tech cocktail hoping to create a future Savior for the people oppressed by Lennox Corp. Fast forward to now, here I am, standing in front of you, watching as you come to the realization that I am indestructible. I have a mental capacity far beyond your own no matter how many Nano-tech injections you get. I am everything Lennox Corp has been trying to create, I am one of a kind and you are on my list! So earlier, when you said I wasn't anything special, you couldn't have been more wrong. I am the walking, talking, indestructible vengeance of the people Lennox Corp has wronged and I will not stop until I deliver a penance that fits their crimes." I saw the last bit of hope drift from his eyes, I had defeated him. His next words were the long awaited payoff, "I will tell you everything I know, just promise me a quick death. No more torture." I agreed to his terms. I told him one last time, "I only need two things: the location of the barge and the codes to access it."

The commander asked me if I was familiar with the coastline, and I produced my old world atlas. A little taken back by the map, he showed me a spot on the coast with a hidden cove. He said pointing at the map, "They anchor the barge there, just offshore. The area will be heavily guarded, and it will take an entire army of men to make it to the water let alone out to the Barge. On top of that, you will need at least 3 people on the barge to activate the chamber that holds the Nano-tech slaves. You must enter 3 separate codes at the same time to gain entry to the chamber. Once in the chamber, the final step to destroy the Nano-tech slave farm will be to inject their feeder tube with a virus that will work its way through the members, killing them within a few minutes." It was unimaginable, thousands of lives lost in an instant. But, I couldn't look at it that way. The Nano-tech people ceased to live when they were hooked up to the machine. I had to think of the countless lives we would save. By the time the Special Commander finished talking, I had not only the codes but more information than I had ever expected. It was obvious not only was he pain intolerant, he figured the more information he gave, the easier I'd go on him in the end. He delivered the supply routes to and from the barge along with extensive details about the size and capabilities of the force protecting the beaches around the cove. He even added information on how the other cities were controlling their slums. Lennox Corp's newest tech was programmed to enslave and dull the senses instead of enhance them. They put it in the water supplies of the slums in S.C.1 and S.C.2. The independent water supply of the S.C.3 slums was the only thing that had saved them so far. So Lennox Corp had to work on a plan to take over in another way, most likely through force. That is why they were increasing their presence and cracking down on people opposing them. They were trying to start a conflict, just as my mother and I had feared, looking for any reason to lock us down and take over. If we had approached this with our original plan, we would have been playing right into the hands of Lennox Corp. Instead we had an abundance of valuable information and had taken one of Lennox Corp's most valuable pieces off the board by removing the Special Commander.

I approached the Special Commander, looked him deep in his eyes and reminded him of the bunker he dropped on Cloud 9. As I did, I gripped his skull with both hands and began squeezing it. I felt my grip getting tighter and tighter and my fingers punctured the Special Commander's skin. He looked up and begged, reminding me my promise of a quick death. Promises be damned, I thought to myself. As I felt the bone compress under the weight of my grip, the blood ran down the sides of his face. Ultimately, I heard a crack, and he died instantly as the splinters entered his brain. I pulled his body down off of the rack and took it outside to burn. I wasn't taking any chances that the Nano-tech could put him back together. His time had come, and I spared him the level of punishment that he in fact deserved. I should have kept him alive for months and made him regret every move he ever made for Lennox Corp. But, the beast itself was in my sights and there was no more time to waste. With the information I now possessed, it was time to build an army of my own. We had to shut Lennox Corp down for good. I now realized that I had been preparing for this my entire life without even knowing it. Now that Claire and I were building an army of supporters, it was up to me to bring us all together.

CHAPTER 15

Blueprints

I cleaned up my bunker and immediately began packing a travel bag. I didn't know when I was coming back. There were a few things I wanted to have with me this time. I had two modified Lennox Corp 40 caliber pistols, along with a .50 caliber sniper rifle with self ranging technology and bullet velocity modifications. I definitely wanted my custom made tomahawks. The blacksmith had made them for me in my early days combing the Wasteland. They were light mobile and never lost their edge. Using them would be another blow from the blacksmith. I gathered the explosives I had been stockpiling over the years. There was no telling what we would need to defeat the security force protecting the cove. One thing was certain, the forces would be Nano-tech enhanced and equipped with the best Lennox Corp weapons. I'm guessing they will have low recoil, high speed repeating rifles with bullet lock technology. Hopefully, once I meet up with Claire, we can put our minds together and develop a plan to destroy that barge. I knew the location and had a good idea of the size of the security force, but we would be blind once we got on the barge. We had no thumb drive and no blueprints. We still needed a way to disable the automated security guns and navigate the barge to find the Tech slaves.

I packed my supplies into an old pickup truck that I kept around for emergencies. It was a relic of the old world, with no tech! Luckily it seems to run fine on moonshine and I have cases of the stuff appropriated from Wasteland bandits. I was only a few miles outside of the slums. I normally hike in, but something was 4telling me to have my entire arsenal ready. I returned to the slums and to my surprise there was no Lennox Corp. security presence. I worried that the Special Commander coming up missing might cause a lockdown or at least increase the security. I took my truck with the supplies to Laura's garage and stashed them there. I picked up Smith while I was there, too. I couldn't believe it, but I had really missed him and you could tell he had missed me. Laura said some scrap rippers had tried to scale the wall one night, looking for an easy score. He wounded one severely. They found the second one dead in the alley a few hours later. He had done his job. He protected Laura and didn't attack anybody innocent.

Smith and I made our way over to Tammy's seeing if my mother was around. Tammy didn't seem surprised to see me, but then again she never did. She immediately asked me, "What did you do?" "Lennox Corp pulled their entire security team from the slums and locked down the city." I said, "Let's just put it this way, the Special Commander has been removed from the equation permanently." She told me she had never seen Lennox Corp act so vulnerable. My mother and I had executed the perfect plan. A strike from the inside had shook things up. We have our slums back, for now. Organizing an uprising of the people and forming a team to take out Lennox Corp will be much easier without the corporation breathing down our necks. My excitement was short lived, as Tammy still had more to tell me. While driving Lennox Corp out of the slums was a great unforeseen side effect of killing the Special Commander, I now had a new more personal problem to worry about. According to Tammy, my mother was in the city trying to secure the blueprints to the barge from a contact she had inside the engineering branch of Lennox Corp. Claire was now trapped inside with the city locked down. There was no way I was getting back inside after recent events. I just had to trust that she knew what she was doing and could get herself out of there once she got her hands on those blueprints.

I headed over to Larry's shop to have him put the word out that anyone who wants a chance to take down Lennox Corp could meet at Tammy's tomorrow night. I knew being this bold would probably bring a few spies to the meeting, but I didn't care. Let them tell Lennox Corp we are organizing. They don't believe we are capable of a revolution let alone realize we know about the barge and intend to destroy it. In their overconfident mindset, they assumed we did not know of the barge. That is why getting back that thumb drive brought the Special Commander into play from the beginning. The barge is a place about which people tell stories, but nobody really believes it exists unless you can prove it to them. I had no intentions of mentioning the barge. This is a call to action to take advantage of the Lennox Corp security force falling back into the city. If the citizens of the slums could make it difficult for Lennox Corp security forces to re-enter the slums, it should buy us the time needed to put together a plan to attack the barge. It shocked Larry to see me. "I heard you were dead!" he said with a chuckle. "Thought the Special Commander dropped a bunker on your head. At least that was the rumor." I replied to him with sarcasm in my voice, "Rumors have a way of proving themselves false more often than not." He got a good laugh out of that one as I knew he would. Rumors are part of his line of work. I told him what I wanted to do, and he was quick to remind me   he was neutral and didn't want trouble. But, he would happily put the word out for the right price. Same old Larry, I had come prepared. I had off loaded the Special Commander's credits during the interrogation process. It was only fair since he wiped me out back at the Cloud 9 bunker. I had to use them within 48 hours, before Lennox Corp suspended them. After the transfer, I let Larry know he could remain neutral, but that all information, about both sides, was to pass through me. After checking his new Credit balance he seemed more than happy to oblige.

I swung back by Tammy's and let her know to prepare for a crowd tomorrow night. I was hoping for a solid turn out. We needed to build a 20 to 30 man unit to keep Lennox Corp from trying to re-enter the slums. The next step was setting up fortifications at all the entry points. I went to each of the three points and measured the entrance then headed over to see Laura. I began gathering up the scrap to fashion the fortifications. They didn't have to be fancy just a deterrent, something to make it clear we were separating ourselves from them and making a stand. If nothing else, they would have to regroup and get approval for a forced entry, hostile takeover. With the Special

Commander out of the picture, it could take the board weeks to decide on something of that magnitude. Now that I knew they were preparing to make a move on rival corporations, over extending their forces, this became the perfect time to hit the barge since they were fighting wars on every front.

I began moving the scrap into piles near the entry points. Help would be needed to build the barriers, but I fully expected to have an entire team behind me come this time tomorrow. After setting up build sites at all the entry points I returned to Laura's. She had been working all day welding materials together to reinforce their strength at the entry sites. Once again she was proving herself to be a worthy replacement for the blacksmith. As I was finishing up my day and getting ready to return to Tammy's for the evening Smith ran off towards the South entry point to the city. He had yet to run off in our time together. I feared for the safety of anybody he might come across on his way to wherever he was going. I followed behind him trying to keep up as he cut down alleyways at a furious pace. Once he reached the south entry point, he sat down at the entrance and peered through to the other side of the Lennox Corp gate. He was not growling or acting protective just watching. And then, out of the shadows a figure appeared; it was my mother. She had been hiding out near the gate for days waiting for someone to come and help her over. I would have to override the gate and shut down the electric razor wire. I had a jammer back at Tammy's. Even with the jammer, you had less than a minute before the power restored, and it fried you. Let's not forget, the razor wire was still razor wire, electrified or not. I headed straight for Tammy's and got the jammer. It occurred to me that I had seen a large metal shelving structure that might prop up against the fence like a ladder. I had to get to the top and cut out a small section of wire. I returned to the gate and propped the shelf up against it. We had 45 seconds, give or take, depending on how quick the reboot kicked in at the gate. She had fashioned a very clever rope ladder for her side. She had not wasted her time while waiting for someone to discover her. I've been so busy I may never have found her if it weren't for Smith. He must have smelled her and knew she needed our help. I climbed up slowly and made sure not to touch the razor wire once I reached the top. I didn't need to get knocked on my ass like the Special Commander. I hit the jammer and cut the wire then Claire threw me her rope ladder. She climbed and I pulled; every second was valuable. As she reached the top, I could feel the internal clock in my head telling me it was close. Just as I pulled her through the opening in the wire, the power came back on. The razor wire surged once again. I smiled at her as we made our way down to the ground on our side of the gate. "Tell me all that was worth it," I said to her in a very concerned tone. Then from under her coat she presented me with a file containing real paper blueprints of the barge. Not some altered digital fakes, these were the original blueprints. I couldn't believe my eyes. I had never seen blueprints for something that indeed existed. I had only found vintage blueprints from the old world. This was painting a picture of how long these corporations had truly been around. I now knew Lennox Corp had been lying about the world beyond the Wasteland. What troubled me is what else they were lying about. How could we believe anything they had taught us? Everything we knew came from Lennox Corp; the year, the rules, the stories about the fall. Everything was now up for speculation, and after this was all over I would cross the ends of the Earth to find the answers. But for now it was time to devise a plan. The blueprints have sealed the deal.

CHAPTER 16

Growing Numbers

My excitement to have my mother back in the slums and the acquisition of the blueprints made it impossible for me to sleep, so I stayed up all night studying the documents. It was likely they had made changes to the barge since the original design. Finding a weak point to the barge should still be possible with the structural integrity all laid out in the blueprints. You could change cosmetic features and add security, but altering a vessel like that structurally was impossible if you still wanted it to float.

The only city that really mattered now was S.C. 1. That was where the board members lived and where they had located the headquarters for Lennox Corp. After destroying the barge we needed to act quickly and take the city securing all labs and destroying all traces of Nano-tech. I was hoping for a big turnout from the information I had Larry put out there, but we would still need the cooperation of Captain Chip in the slums of S.C. 1. If I could get him to mobilize his people, and be ready to move on the city as soon as he hears from me, that would give us immediate boots on the ground after the destruction of the barge. I went out to the lounge and asked Tammy to get a message to Captain Chip. All I could do now was wait and hope for a fast response. I headed out to get a feel for the mood of the slums, and to my surprise over 20 people were already at Tammy's waiting for me. I gathered them up and showed them the fortifications we must build. "When we finish, we will meet back at Tammy's and I will explain everything," I said.

I started the people fortifying the entrances from the inside and preparing for Lennox Corp's efforts to re-enter the slums. As the day continued more and more people kept showing up. Each group seemed more eager than the last to join the cause. I was now seeing how oppressed the people felt by Lennox Corp. Each one of them is ready to take back their lives from the overbearing corporation. I guess I had spent so much time in the Wasteland only thinking about myself, I couldn't see the pot primed for a boil-over. The more people that showed up, the more inspired I felt. I could now understand my mother's belief in my purpose. This wasn't about destroying Lennox Corp; this was about freeing people from tyranny. We worked hard on the defenses and I let my mind work on the blueprints, still hoping to find a weakness. Claire had isolated herself after returning with the blueprints. I didn't know why, but I also did not know what she had to do to get them.

Re-entering the city for the first time in a long time must have brought about its own demon's, too. I felt she was withholding large portions of the truth, and I was fine with that for now. I had much more important things on my plate.

I found it odd that Lennox Corp had remained locked down with no attempt to establish contact or re-establish a security presence. I couldn't have scared them that bad. Something else had to be going on. I was hoping to get some answers once I heard from Captain Chip. After a hard day's work transforming the slums into a giant fortress, I returned to my room and once again began studying the blueprints of the barge. The barge was at least 400 yards long and contained many confusing corridors that crisscrossed as you traversed through the multiple levels. According to the digital data I had originally seen, thanks to the sacrifice of Cloud 9, there were automated turrets on the top deck. These turrets use thermal imaging to lock onto vehicles or humans up to a mile away. But as you enter the lower decks, there was no security at all. I didn't believe for one minute Lennox Corp was short-sighted enough to think the turrets were enough protection. I was counting on human patrols on those lower decks and my goal was to avoid them at all cost. There was a large, enclosed space in the barge's belly, and that was my target room. It measured 200 yards long with reinforcement. My head's telling me this has to be the Nano-slave server room, but the boat's hull seemed impenetrable. No matter how I looked at these blueprints I couldn't find a weakness. The barge appeared to be robustly guarded and structurally sound. Even with my Nano-tech intelligence, I was stumped. I wanted to give the blueprints to my mother and let her have a crack at them, but with her in self-imposed isolation I compromised and took them over to Laura. No harm in a fresh pair of eyes checking my dilemma. I sat down with her and explained how I needed to get to the area in the hull to destroy the Nano-farm, and how all of it hinged on my ability to enter the boat. She seemed as excited as I was to see real blueprints and promptly began scanning the documents. She asked if I could give her some time, so I left with the blueprints and returned to Tammy's.

The crowd continued to grow and had gathered, ready to hear the plan to take down Lennox Corp. I needed to lay it out for them in a way that only included their role to play. The knowledge of the barge would only serve to confuse the people and alert spies for Lennox Corp. I silenced the room and delivered a speech. "You have all come here to tear down the illusion that Lennox Corp has created and for the first time that possibility is real. We have them scared; they have retreated into their city. But mark my words, we will grow in numbers and march on their city making it our city. But, make no mistake; the citizens within those walls will be freed as well. They are just like you and have been manipulated by the corporation to believe the propaganda being fed to them daily. I have seen it with my own eyes. They are just waiting for us, the people of the slums, to rise up and free them. Only we possess the courage that they have long since lost. We have survived the Lennox Corp regime and come out of the other side stronger and more determined. Now with all of us here today, ready to stand up and fight for true freedom, a society of truth will emerge. Each one of you must protect these slums with your life because we will build the future society in the people's image of freedom not the corporation's. The corporate control must end, Lennox Corp must fall!" After getting everyone fired up and ready for the task at hand, I delegated security details to patrol our walls and fortifications. I then put the rest to work organizing our supplies and weapons. If we had everything already prepared, it would be easier to strike when the time arrived. Once we destroyed the barge and network, there was no telling what kind of resistance Lennox Corp would present to protect the cities. The crowd dispersed as everyone headed off to fulfill their delegated tasks. As they did, I noticed one person sitting across the room; it was my mother.

I had not noticed Claire amongst the crowd. "Nice speech, I see you finally understand what is at stake." She said, "I apologize for my absence. I have some difficult intelligence to share with you". She told me her contact shared information with her on the current state of Lennox Corp. The contact has a theory that the Lennox Corp board has been dissolved, and the corporation is being run by outside forces. It seems board members only mingled with board members and no one has seen a single board member for years. I had heard this over the last few years but never gave it much thought. She admitted she had heard the same over the years, but didn't believe it until now. The person telling her this was the same person from whom she collected the blueprints; a trusted friend. The problem was, he, like anyone else, was just speculating. No one had any sure way to know. I told my mother, "My thought is, once we shut down their barge and march into the city and right into their boardroom someone will be sitting there. Whoever that person may be will answer my questions and pay the price. In my experience someone always runs the show. Puppets cannot exist without a master to control them and someone or some group of people have spent a long time turning us into puppets." I couldn't believe that any controlling group of individuals, especially enhanced individuals, would walk away from such a huge investment of time and resources. No way. The strings were being manipulated somehow and the responsible party or parties would be held accountable. She agreed with me but something still seemed off about her and given her gift for hiding pieces of the truth I could only assume that wasn't the only thing bothering her. I asked her if there was anything else she needed to tell me and her answer was "It will all be revealed when it should be." That was not very reassuring considering we were well under way in coordinating an invasion on multiple fronts, and would be blowing up the barge as soon as we could find a penetration point. I expressed my eagerness to have all the facts, but she said, "I have more legwork to do and will be back when the time is right." She stocked up on supplies and headed out into the Wasteland, unwilling to tell me where she was going or for what purpose she was going. Her last words were "The people are yours now protect them." It felt like goodbye for good, but something inside me knew that just wasn't true. We would see each other again. She wouldn't leave me to fight this fight alone, that much I knew. There had to be something she found out that would put us at an even greater risk if it was true. I just didn't know what that could be. This was her way and all I could do was let her go. Whatever she was doing, it was to help us walk the path of freedom and that was all that really mattered. I couldn't help but watch as she disappeared into the Wasteland. It felt like every time I got close to her and the chance to find out more about myself, she would distance herself from me. In her defense these were extenuating circumstances and my mind might have been clouded by my own selfish thoughts of learning about who I really am.

As I turned to make my way back to Tammy's, Smith ran off in an excited fit, and that only meant one thing; Laura was close by. Sure enough, from around the corner here she came, beaming from ear to ear. I could already tell she had found a way inside the barge. I followed her back to the garage where she had pinned the blueprints up on the walls so she could see them all at the same time. She came right out with it! Even though she could tell I already knew, she maintained her excitement. "I figured it out!" She said with intense and focused joy. "I only have one condition before I give you this information," She said as her tone became considerably more serious. "I come with you and we do the job together. It is a two-person job and I am the only one qualified, and the only one you can trust to not tuck tail and run if this goes bad." I reluctantly agreed to her terms. Laura was becoming one of a handful of people I genuinely trusted. Also, having her there would make me a lot more comfortable. You match that with her knowledge of metal and the fact that she had figured out in an evening something that had eluded me; it was obvious she was the only choice. My path continued to reveal itself. I now had a way on to the barge and growing numbers for the invasion and overthrow of the city. Lennox Corp now existed on borrowed time.

CHAPTER 17

Putting It All Together

Laura and I sat down. She proceeded to explain her plan to me, and it was a masterpiece. Under the primary hull where we expected the Nano-slaves to be, she located a compact space between the hull of the boat and the room holding the Nano-slaves. Her plan was to dive underneath the boat and cut into that compartment. I get in as quickly as possible and she seals it back up letting in only minimal water. I then use the cutting torch to get into the room from underneath undetected. If I'm entering the Nano-tech farm chamber directly through the hull instead of through the chamber door, I won't need 3 people to deactivate the chamber. Once in, I should be able to inject the feeder tubes with the Nano-virus and plant the explosives myself. Maneuvering between the decks appears to be the trickiest part; I needed to get myself to the 5th deck which houses the outflow vents for air intake and cooling ducts to the outside. I was hoping to ride my way right off the boat and into the water before the explosion. My Nano-tech brain was memorizing every inch of the blueprints. I only have 10 minutes to make it out before the explosives detonate. I fully expect security patrols on each of the floors so getting lost was not an option. This needed to be a low key operation; just myself, Laura and Smith. The Special Commander stated the area around the cove was thick with vegetation and heavily patrolled. It also provided high ground from several locations around the beach. If Smith creates a distraction, maybe takes out a few of the patrols, Laura and I would have more time to slip onto the beach and get the boat in the water, hopefully unnoticed. I wish I were doing this alone, but the blacksmith taught Laura all about underwater welding and I knew nothing. Luckily, I have experience with the torch I'll be using to cut through the floor. But the underwater stuff required skills I did not possess. Besides, I gave her my word.

I returned to Tammy's knowing that we had a way onto the ship. I still needed to decide the best way to approach the beach. When I walked into Tammy's, a messenger from Captain Chip was waiting to talk to me. He brought me news that Captain Chip should arrive in two days. I didn't understand how that was possible until the messenger told me that Lennox Corp had also pulled the security forces from the slums of S.C. 1, leaving Captain Chip in charge. Lennox Corp's reaction seemed extreme. This was too much activity to be a result from the loss of the Special Commander of S.C. 3. There had to be something else going on here. Lennox Corp was making a move. The question was to what extent? I thanked the messenger and had Tammy set him up with a place to stay until Captain Chip arrived. Finally, I was in my room. I sat quietly, organizing my moves. My ability to maximize the information I had learned would directly affect our success. This was the big move. We couldn't afford to miss our opportunity; we may only get the one. As Smith and I entered our room, I noticed a box sitting over on the table. I opened it and inside was a note from my mother that said, "Tristan, enclosed is my last Nano-tech shot. I left it for you in case you need it. Good Luck Son. I believe in you". I thought about throwing the shot away, when a better idea occurred to me. The bond I was building with Smith was definitely growing and his speed and strength were unmatched. If this shot developed his intelligence to the point of understanding complex commands, and extend his life expectancy, I would have a dependable sidekick watching my back from now on. I'd like our bond to become more than just a wild dog and his Alpha leader. I looked over at him deciding to give this more thought. If the side effects were deleterious, and he became crazy and unstoppable with rage, that could present a problem.

I needed Captain Chip to have his technician set up an encrypted network for us to use for communication without fear of being detected. Laura, Smith and myself would use the old truck to pull the boat and work our way through the jungle and downward to the beach. Meanwhile, a force of nearly 50 men will hold a position at the edge of the jungle waiting for the signal; the explosion. When that happens, it will draw the Lennox patrols cascading along the beach giving our forces the high ground. They will be easy targets for our men. No matter what their numbers, the element of surprise and strategic posting should make up the difference in our favor. Laura and I should have had enough time by then to make our way around to the other side of the cape and onto the beach. I will then send Captain Chip and Tammy a message on the encrypted network for him and his men to take S.C. 1. Their goal is to kill every member of the board. Meanwhile, Tammy and the forces of our slums could take S.C. 3. After securing two of the 3 cities we could easily remove any level of resistance left over from S.C. 2.

Once Captain Chip arrived, I wanted to call a meeting between Laura, myself, Tammy and Captain Chip. I would outline the plan, open the table for further suggestions and get everyone ready to make our move. Laura and I spent the next couple of days working on our equipment and our stealth boat. It not only needed to get us to the barge, but out of the cove and around the coast to the beach on the other side. We made a frame with a light weight but strong material and put tubing around it, covering it in tough rubber cement. The waterproof adhesive would give it a more solid bond. It will need to stay afloat for a couple of hours. We also built a small engine for the escape. It won't hold much fuel so we will have to cross our fingers that it will finish the job. There was no room for error. If we got too far-off the coast and sucked out to sea, we were finished. Laura had rigged an insulated pack designed to hold her underwater welding rig. She estimated 10 minutes to gear up, another 5 to get in place. The weld itself may take as much as half an hour. She needed me to man the radio from up top in case a problem should arise. It was becoming apparent how dangerous this was for her. I was tasked with manning the boat and watching for patrols. Once she radioed me that she was ready, I had to be ready to jump in and make my way to her. I had to be ready the minute she made the breach to limit the amount of water bleeding in with me. I highly doubted that I would even need my breathing apparatus, but I took it in case the space filled up with water faster than expected. Laura estimated it could take me a half hour to an hour to cut through the floor. I hoped that was an overestimation. Cramped half an hour or more in a tight space between the hull of a boat and the room above didn't sound like a lot of fun.

When I left Laura, she was back tinkering with the escape boat. I said goodbye and headed out into the slums to make my rounds and check the entrances. Morale was high, but everyone I spoke to was definitely on edge anticipating our next move. I reassured everyone that I spoke to; this would be a quick and definitive resolution leading to a better future for us all. Everyone had a role to play and each must remain focused on the task at hand. I returned to Tammy's and decided that I would give Smith the Nano-tech shot and a light sedative while he adjusted to it. The only way this gets done is if Smith can create a big enough distraction for Laura and me to get the boat down to the beach and into the water. We would park the truck at the edge of the jungle.

That would leave us 1/4 mile to traverse across the beach to the water. Once there, we had to move quick, getting the boat in the water and the equipment loaded.

I took Smith back to the room and had him sit. I gave him the sedative and waited for him to lie down. As he lay calm, I injected him with the Nano-tech. He didn't even whimper. He had seen so many battles the shot didn't faze him in the least. I decided not to leave him in case the Nano-tech had an adverse effect on him. He slept for a few hours and when he woke up, you could already tell the Nano-tech had interfaced with him successfully. He immediately sat up with a calm and focused presence about him. I tested the extent of the effects of the Nano-tech. My first command, "Go get Laura". To my elation, he returned moments later with Laura right behind him. She said he practically pushed her the first few feet. Next, I scratched a quick note to Larry asking him if he had heard anything on the Lennox Corp side of things and told Smith to deliver it. Amazingly, he sure as hell did, returning a few minutes later with the predictable response of no. I still didn't believe Larry knew which side he belonged on. I think he is afraid that if Lennox Corp credits go away, then so does his usefulness, but in reality there will always be a barter system. After Smith passed the first couple of tests, I told him to run off to the main gate and wait for Captain Chip, then come get me when he shows up.

Captain Chip we be arriving soon, so I started gathering everyone up. I wanted to come out and relay the plan to the people, immediately after the meeting of the leaders. I revealing the plan, it would be more about delegating manpower and assigning battle tasks. The details of the plan would remain between the 4 people in the meeting. I swung back by checking in on Laura's progress with the boat, and not surprising to me at all, she was nearly done. Even better, the boat itself only weighed around 150 pounds. With the equipment and the explosives we would be carrying around 275 pounds. It looks like we will need two more people to help carry the boat if we want to make decent time and remain un-detected. Not the news I wanted, but we needed this boat and the supplies. I was hoping to impose on Captain Chip, yet again, once he got here. He had men he trusted, and I needed to borrow two of them to help Laura and I navigate the jungle and get the boat and supplies to the beach fast. I needed two guys with a sound track record of loy-alty to Captain Chip.

While talking this through, Laura came up with a brilliant idea. Her proposal was that we load the boat with the equipment and lower it with a guide rope and a parachute, off the side of the cliff behind the barge. That way, the barge itself would obstruct the view from the beach, keeping us out of site. We then use the climbing gear to get down to the water and pull the boat to us with the rope. I loved it; no Nano-tech and yet another plan made better from her contribution. More and more I observed why she was so special to the blacksmith. She said, "I can rig a slight charge to detonate remotely, releasing an anchor when the boat hits the water. The anchor will keep the boat from getting too far away while we climbed down the cliff to the water." The cliff only measured 60 ft or so high on the map. Then she said, "The parachute should be able to stabilize the craft as it falls through the air and we would have the guide rope to help guide it and keep it upright." This alternative plan was a game changer. We no longer need an entire beach of soldiers to fall for a distraction and Smith could concentrate on navigate the jungle, taking out any patrols getting too close. Finally, we had put it all together and just in time. Smith came running in to Laura's shop alerting me that Captain Chip had arrived.

CHAPTER 18

Meeting of the Minds

I headed over to the primary entrance to greet Captain Chip and his men. It was apparent he had a lot on his mind. I hoped to ease this as quickly as possible. The first words out of his mouth were, "I expected you to be dead. Then Lennox Corp pulls out of the slums, and I hear it's because the Special Commander has disappeared. Not too long after, a messenger delivers a note from said dead man. If I'm doing the math right, you must be the one responsible for the Special Commander's disappearance." I assured him that everything will make more sense after I get everyone together. He was in a hurry to return to his slums as he felt they were in some kind of danger.

He had only come because he was in disbelief that I was alive and looking to overthrow Lennox Corp. A lot had happened, and a lot had changed since the last interaction I had with him so I understood his concern. I showed him over to Tammy's and when we got there, Laura sat waiting for us. Tammy had cleared out the bar and the guest rooms. She did one last sweep and locked the entire place down. I stood at the end of the table surrounded by Laura, Tammy, Captain Chip and the men Captain Chip had brought along. I suggested I begin with my plan and its applications, and then I would open up the floor for questions, or further suggestions. To start the meeting, Laura and I went back over our plan to navigate the jungle, traverse the cliff and boat out to the barge where we would enter the ship from underneath. The only detail I left out being my knowledge of the Nano-tech and the farm. I didn't need anyone panicked because the other side has enhanced capabilities. The Nano-tech would give those troops an advantage; it will destroy them. The Nano-tech wasn't in me. It was me and the patrols couldn't account for that no matter how many shots they received. I turned to Tammy, "It would honor me if you led the attack on S.C. 3. You will lead the people to begin the attack as soon as you hear the explosion of the barge. I trust you to understand that we will free the people enslaved by the city and eliminate the ones controlling it. Also, it will be very important having you in charge to gauge when about a third of the fighters from here in S.C.3 can march on to S.C. 1 to back up Captain Chip and myself. Captain Chip's people will lock down the high-rise where the board members are housed. Once we blow those doors, it will be a fight to the top floor and the board-room. We will need all the able body fighters we can get before we breach." Tammy accepted her role to lead the people of S.C.3 with pride.

Next, I needed to go over the part of the

plan that involved Captain Chip. So much had transpired since we last met. I told him the barge was real, and we had a plan to blow it up, giving us an opportunity to take all three cities and overthrow Lennox Corp. I knew he would want to know how we intended to destroy the barge and how we got so much information about its location. So I shared with him, I was the one that forced the cities into lockdown, as he had expected. I told him about how I had snuck into the city and had taken the Special Commander hostage forcing the information out of him through interrogation. I said, "I will need you and your men to take S.C. 1, forcing a lockdown and trapping the Lennox Corp board members in the corporate headquarters building. If you can hold there for 3 days while awaiting mine and Laura's return, we will bring our forces with us and blow the security doors and storm the building, ultimately executing the board members." I then expressed how I needed his technician to set up an encrypted network to use for private communication. I concluded, "I will also need two sturdy guys, preferably from your personal security, to help us get the boat and the supplies to the cliff." After I finished laying it all out I gave captain Chip the floor. I figured he would have several questions and possibly a few objections.

He started off in a defiant tone, "None of this will work and you are asking me to sacrifice my people. You still haven't told me how you are still alive or why you suddenly care about taking down Lennox Corp. You only care about the credits. If you are still alive and those kids from Cloud 9 are dead, that means you sold them out when things got too thick. I trusted you to step up." He stated bitterly, "You tell me how you survived without selling out those kids and if I believe you, you will have my support." I still didn't feel comfortable sharing information about Nano-tech with him. I looked around conscious of the support that came

with both Laura and Tammy in the room. I needed
a story, minus the Nano-tech and I hoped Laura
and Tammy would follow my lead. One day I
wanted to tell Captain Chip the truth about Nano-
tech, but the image of being able to extend your
life or gaining superior power had a way of corrupting people and blurring their vision. I needed
everyone clear headed and focusing on the removal of Lennox Corp. And so I began, "I was in the
bunker and the entire thing was a trap. The Special Commander had been one step ahead of me
the entire time while we were trying to access the
hard drive. I assumed I was manipulating the Special Commander but actually, he was manipulating me." I explained to him every slow motion
second I could recall of the time in the bunker.
Now it was time to color outside the lines, because we always base the best lies in truth. I continued, "By a freak bit of luck, I survived. Two
metal beams had collapsed, bending into each
other creating a shelter for holding back the ma-

jority of the rubble and fire. When I came to, I remember enduring a desperate climb through the rubble. It seems Laura found me unable to walk and barely alive about 50 feet from the explosion site, laying near a dumpster where she was looking for scrap metal. Laura and Tammy were listening intently shaking their heads in agreement. She took me to Tammy where they hid me out in her cutaway basement where she stores the liquor." I told him that once I was healthy enough, I headed out into the Wasteland and came up with the plan for entering the city and killing the Special Commander. "Once in the city, I followed the commander, captured him and brought him out via the outflow pipes." He now had enough information. He must decide if he's on board or not. Reality is, he really doesn't have a choice. The war is coming whether or not he helps us. Our way would be the only way we came out on top. I wrapped our talk up by saying, "I will give you some time to consider what I've said. I respect you

and we need you but only if you want to be here."
Laura and Tammy had once again proven their
loyalty and their friendship by bearing silent wit-
ness to the story I told Captain Chip. While Captain Chip sat inside deciding about his involvement, I called the people together to make an an-
nouncement. The time had come to tell everyone,
in one week from today Lennox Corp would no
longer rule our world.

The people gathered as they had before,
once again expecting a speech. There appeared no
fear in their eyes for what I was proposing here
today. I was observing sheer determination and
belief; determination to take back their lives and
the belief in me to help them do so. I would not
disappoint them. I would not let them down. Lennox Corp had its time. Now is the time of the
People. I stood up in front of everyone and let my
passion guide the speech. "One week from today
you will look at the person beside you right now

and they will not be the same person you see today. They will be someone that none of us imagined we could ever be. They will be a human being, free from the tyranny of corporate rule. They will be an independent thinker, ready to shape the future world in their own image of freedom. As you look at them notice them looking at you with the same level of admiration. You know why, because you too will be that human being. This isn't just a fight; this is a movement. A victory against Lennox Corp isn't simply a new life, it's a new world. Now, I want all of you to remember who you are and why you are fighting because Lennox Corp is not going to roll over. What they don't recognize is there is nothing they can do to stop us because they created us. Every time they deprived us of water all they did was make us stronger. Every time they rationed our food, they made us stronger. Every time they pushed us down and worked us to the bone in the mines we just got stronger. That is what they couldn't see coming. They built our strength and now our movement is a juggernaut that will not stop." After an eruption of cheers, I followed the speech by sharing the leaders of the groups. "These are your Leaders with the city attack plan. One week from now you will receive an order from Tammy to attack S.C. 3. Their defenses will be down. You are to eliminate security personnel that pose a threat. Please try not to harm the cities citizens. Lennox Corp enslaved them just as they enslaved you. After securing the city, Tammy will delegate a third of you to rendezvous with myself and hopefully Captain Chip to assist in the overthrow of S.C. 1." Before I another word left my lips, Captain Chip popped out from within the crowd. He announced. "I listened to your speech, and I contemplated the tragedy that unfolded with you and Cloud9, and I trust you and give you my full support. I just hope everyone here knows and fully understands what we are about to do. We will suffer heavy casualties no matter how perfect the plan. And those that survive will have to live knowing the many that we lost." I completely understood his position. If he only knew how many casualties I was expecting and what I had to do on that barge it would disgust him. To be honest, it disgusted me. But no matter how many times I weigh the options, the conclusion came out the same. The only acceptable outcome would be the removal of Lennox Corp and, even more importantly, Nano-tech. I thanked him for his support and went back over all the plans with him again. By the time we had finished, he seemed comfortable with the plan and believed we had about as good of a chance of success as you might expect with so many moving parts. Tammy put him and his men up for the night. Captain Chip and his men were headed straight back to S.C. 1 slums in the morning to prepare the people and get his technicians to work on our encrypted network. He introduced me to the two men that would accompany Laura and me to the barge. Both were big, burly guys with broad shoulders. The first man he introduced me to was Tim, a very stern man who specialized in knives and hand to hand combat. The next man was Riker, a former Lennox Corp security agent cast out for exposing a smuggling scam being run by a few of his fellow agents. Lennox Corp had put him through all levels of their training, making him proficient in all weaponry. Here was another ex-citizen and employee of Lennox Corp that did not realize their vitamin injections contained Nano-tech. They likely enhanced him to some level, and he didn't even notice it. Everything had come together, the plan of attack, the leaders I had chosen, and the people of the slums. I would finish making preparations here and soon follow Captain Chip to S.C. 1. He would need two days to get things set up on his end. With the meeting of the minds done, it was time to act.

CHAPTER 19

The Jungle

L aura and I spent the next couple of days loading all of our supplies and preparing the convoy. At the pace we would move with a convoy this size it should take us 4 days to reach the slums of S.C. 1, where we would link up with Tim and Riker and head for the coast. The coast was approximately 2 days from S.C. 1 if we drove straight through the night. Our forces would stage at the edge of the jungle awaiting our signal; the explosion of the barge. The cliff where we wanted to drop the boat in the water, would be about another 2.5 mile hike up. Only about 1.5 miles of it was trail after that we would lug a boat down a path cleared by a machete. Not a simple task, but still better than taking the risk of alerting the forces guarding the barge. If they were to see us coming, they would lock the barge down, and no plan would get us inside. The travel to the slums of S.C. 1 went like a breeze. With everything turned upside down, the Wasteland seemed like a ghost town. I met up with Captain Chip and he again warned me of the consequences if we failed, and I quickly reminded him we must succeed. Shortly after talking with the captain, Tim and Riker made their way to the convoy. I thanked them again and explained to them the importance of their roles. Everyone seemed eager to get started, so we decided to push on through the night.   We could camp once we reached the coastal jungle.

Traffic, pedestrian or vehicle, did not frequent the road to the coast. It was a harsh and unforgiving place protected by a fierce, thick jungle. No one was sure just how many creatures, let alone what nature of creatures, inhabited the jungle. No one who journeyed to the coast ever returned. Now that we were aware of what Lennox Corp was hiding out here, we surmised not only dangerous animals have been at work, so have the Lennox patrols. I have never even been to the edge of the jungle. The coast never interested me. Crossing through miles of hostile jungle to lay eyes on an enormous body of water didn't sound like an enjoyable time to me. Soon I would find out why so many sacrificed their lives to catch a glimpse of the ocean. The convoy pushed hard, and we made the jungle in 36 hours. We built a base camp about 2 miles from the edge of the jungle. This would be the staging area for the force that would take the cliffs and remove the security force from the beach. The four of us going into the jungle would continue on the path until we hit the deviation point where we would have to create our own path. The main path was a Lennox Corp supply route and heavily patrolled as you got closer to the beach, according to the Special Commander. Unfortunately we had no other choice. It would have taken far too long to cut an entire new path. The part we had to cut was already too much as far as I was concerned. It was time for Smith to show off his new enhancement. I sat him down, looked him in the eye, pointed out the path and said "Clear the path boy, no surprises. I want a threat free trip to the deviation point." He immediately darted off down the path. A level of security came with Smith out ahead of us clearing the way. You could traverse the path, but it still presented many obstacles while carrying a boat and supplies. It didn't take us 20 minutes to stumble upon some of Smith's handy work. He killed a 4 man patrol and dragged them off the path into the woods. My confidence continued to grow. We will cut through this jungle, launch this boat and destroy that barge. We made it to the deviation point with no incidents thanks to Smith's excellent work. We put the boat down and Riker and Laura sat on watch while Tim and I began cutting our path to the coastal cliffs. The boat didn't need to be moved until we cleared the entire path. It was easier to defend your position if you weren't dropping a boat in the middle of the small path you just created. Plus, clearing the path first allowed us to check the area around the path for predators. As we cut through the foliage, I marveled at the jungle habitat. Luscious deep greens with beautiful flowers everywhere. I had seen nothing like it except in books from the Old World. This was truly amazing. If this all works out as planned, I want to return and explore this vast jungle for treasures. For now I couldn't let my mind wander too much, the more I focused, the faster this path would get cut. After about two hours, Tim returned to the edge of the path and traded places with Riker. Tim had not said a word to me during the entire process. Riker however wouldn't shut up. He immediately had questions. "How are you not tired yet?" he asked in an Alpha male kind of way. I just laughed and responded. "It's mind over matter." He didn't like that answer. He then began asking me why I needed two guys from Captain Chip when I was the glorious leader. "Don't you have anybody you can trust?" he said. I responded, "Yes I do. She is sitting at the edge of this path we are cutting, keeping watch." He then came back again, "Oh I see, just you and the misses. I get it." This was getting old fast, and I didn't have time for small talk. I cut this conversation off short. "Let's just cut the path," I stated with authority in my voice. He sarcastically replied, "You are the boss." I might have hurt his feelings or pissed him off, but at least the work advanced in silence.

We continued cutting until we heard a rustling off in the bushes to the right about 20 yards into the jungle and moving fast right at us. I heard a distinct snorting noise, and I immediately knew it was a pack of wild boars pushing us to assert dominance over their territory; we didn't belong.

From their flank, I saw another shape moving through the thick jungle heading straight for the lead boar. Then a loud aggressive tussle ensued between the pack of boars and the mystery animal. Riker and I stayed ready, weapons in hand. After the commotion settled, a large silhouette came jogging out of the jungle holding something in its mouth. As it got closer a smile covered my face. It was Smith carrying the head of one of the wild boars. He brought it to me placing it right at my feet. I thanked him and rewarded him with a strip of salted beef. I told him, "Go back to work boy." He immediately ran off, disappearing into the thick jungle. Riker and I got back to work. He said, "That is the most badass dog I have ever seen." Riker and I finally agreed about something. By my estimation we had cut only about a half mile of jungle in 8 hours of non-stop work. At this pace, we still had another 8 hours of clearing left to do. Riker left after a few hours, and Laura returned in his place. I had not taken a break except to eat some strips of salted beef. Once Laura joined the effort, things moved a little faster. Her effort level was much higher than either Tim or Riker's had been. We had about two or three more solid hours at the current pace and we would lay eyes on the ocean. Laura and I talked about what we would do after we destroyed Lennox Corp. I told her what I had learned about the other corporations and there being an immense world out there past the Wasteland. She seemed as interested as I did in exploring the world beyond what we had always known. As we continued talking, a future beyond Lennox Corp emerged. I stopped for a moment and looked back at Laura, "If we survive this and we're successful in taking down Lennox Corp, would you be interested in joining Smith and me in exploring the world beyond here?" Before she answered, I could already see it written on her face that the answer was yes, but I didn't let on. I let her answer for herself. And with an elevated level of energy, given the situation, she responded, "Yes and anything after yes!" I grinned and said, "That's fine, we take this world on together as we move forward." It overjoyed me. I truly believed that with Smith and Laura by my side, anything was possible. As we fantasized about our future adventures, the work continued to fly by and before we knew it, the sun came pouring through the vegetation, signaling that we were close to the edge. We slowed our clearing process to be more methodical. We didn't want to fall off the edge of the cliff because we were in a hurry. After a few minutes of precise clearing the edge presented itself and to be honest the view out over the ocean was the most inspiring thing I had ever seen. I immediately regretted the ignorant point of view I had taken on the ocean for the entirety of my life. I was clearly uneducated on the situation. Laura and I stood there silent, staring out into the open ocean way past the cliff walls of the cove, the turquoise waves drifting endlessly into the horizon.

The beach beyond the barge was not visible from our vantage point, so we still were unable to ascertain the size of the Lennox patrols. I doubted the patrols in the jungle would be an issue if there were even any left alive after Smith finished making his rounds. The barge was everything the blueprints had promised. The largest vessel of any kind I had ever seen by far. It barely even fit in the cove. The automated turrets were more menacing than I had imagined. I didn't even need binoculars. Now that I knew about the other corporations, I could see this level of security was not meant for us; it was in case of attack from another corporation. Laura and I hike back to meet Tim and Riker. We told them we had made it to the cliff edge, and they both seemed elated. The four of us carried the boat full of equipment to the edge of the cliff, attached the parachute to it and threw it over the side. The plan worked beautifully, and the boat glided down to the water and rested upright on top. I sent Tim and Riker back to the base camp to await the signal. Tim and Riker wished us luck and headed back to the path. Laura blew the charge releasing the anchor, and the boat snuggled right up to the edge of the rocks. We couldn't have placed it there any better. Laura and I got our climbing spikes on and got ready to make our descent. I tied her off to a tree just in case. She was not an experienced climber, and losing her was not an option. We made our way down slow and steady. She was a natural, and after only a few brief minutes we were already safely in the boat. We had survived the jungle and launched the boat successfully. It was time to tackle the barge.

CHAPTER 20

The Barge

Laura and I maneuvered our way around behind the barge and positioned our boat as close as possible to where we needed to work. We were like a speck on the side of this thing; it was more of a floating compound than a boat. There was no way they could move this thing even if they had to. That was why it was so well defended with the turrets and the security force. Laura took longer than expected to cut through the outer layer of the hull and ended up using both of our breathing masks. Hopefully, the oxygen in the hole would be sufficient, and my work would progress quickly. I highly doubted I would drown either way, but I didn't want to take any unnecessary chances. I couldn't wait to feel the tug of that line and get started on my part. The sooner I was in the small space the sooner I was out of it. Suddenly, the tug came, and I quickly dove into the water. I could already see that the hole was taking on more water than expected. I swam as fast as I could up inside of it. Laura began welding it shut behind me, but it was too late, the water nearly filled the space. Just as the space took on the last of the water, Laura sealed the hole behind me. I held my breath for as long as I could, struggling to retrieve my respirator. It seemed to be caught on something and I couldn't break it free. I'll know real damn quick if I will drown. As I released my breath, I could feel my body compensating for my environmental surroundings. My vision cleared, and the choking sensation gave way to a new breathing technique. I couldn't believe what was happening. I was breathing and functioning underwater with genuine efficiency. It was looking more and more as though there was nothing in this world that could kill me, and I didn't honestly know how I felt about that prospect. After the water settled into the space, I had a 2in deep by 14 inch long space in which to work. I focused the cutting torch up there. I got to work immediately keeping the flame just out of the water and the heat as high as I could stand it. I developed a pattern 25 minutes on and 10 minutes off. I brought a thermite torch in case my primary torch got water logged.   The Lennox Corp thermite cutting torch was one of the most versatile, compact cutting torches I have ever used. My preparation had paid off as the water took its toll and I had to switch over. This was taking longer than expected. After over 2 hours of work, I finally cut a section just big enough to squeeze through with the explosives and the virus injections. My duffle of weapons would remain behind.

I shimmied up through the opening with just what I needed, and just as Laura had thought,

I was inside of a service room connected to the Nano-slave holding area. The room doubled as storage. I saw charts, records and supplies but unfortunately, no weapons. As I opened the door and proceeded out into the area beyond, I wasn't sure I could believe what I was looking at, and then it all came into focus. There were rows and rows of people as far as the eye could see. They were lying in these custom-made chairs, with multiple tubes and lines running in and out of their bodies. Their eyes appeared empty and glassed over. The citizens appeared to be in a deep state of coma, unaware of anything around them, including me. I followed the room, taking notice of the numbers. By the time I reach the end, I lost count of how many people were imprisoned in this hell. My mother had estimated that there would be around 1,000 people. In reality, this was much closer to 5,000 people. Lennox Corp had been at this for a while. Everything that they were projecting and creating was being sent back and forth between all of their minds with some strange routing wire that carried an eerie glow. All the Nano-tech inside of me and I didn't understand any of what I was looking at or how it worked. The setup was an incredibly advanced nightmare. Best I could tell, they were using the brain power of the Nano-slaves to fuse Nano-tech with the servers, but also using them to feed off of each other. They were creating their own network where Nano-tech is perfecting Nano-tech, using the slave's brain as excess storage to access as needed. This was mental slavery on a massive scale. If Nano-tech was manipulating at the level it appeared here, everyone with Nano-tech in them was in danger; including myself. This farm was the proof Nano-tech in the wrong hands was deadly.

There was no sign of a security presence on this level just as we had been told. There were two A.I. robots that came through checking tubes and connections from time to time. I was glad they were around. I wouldn't have known which tube was the feeder tube without seeing the robot adding a vitamin paste down one of the tubes. I took time to evaluate the situation. I wanted to be sure there were no other alternatives before I carried out a plan that included a mass casualty event of otherwise innocent people. It was apparent they nourished the bodies for the sole purpose of housing the brains of the citizens. The true essence of the citizens had long since died. That didn't change the fact that whether they were aware of what was happening to them or not, it still felt wrong. After searching my thoughts, I knew what I must do. As sad as it was, all these people were now a vessel for Nano-tech. This was the breeding ground for all of Lennox Corp's power; Lennox Corp must fall. I watched the robots make their round one more time. I fell in behind, injecting the Nano-virus into the three separate feeding tubes. It was the only way to assure the virus enters the body and brain undetected. I then began setting out the explosives. I didn't know how long it would take for the Nano-virus to take effect, but once it did this entire barge would begin shutting down. Once that happened I would trigger the timer on the explosives and make my way up to deck 5. I had already been scouting the area, as I followed the robots around. The blueprints came into my mind, and the layout appeared making me aware of my location. There was a service compartment that the bots rode up and down in. That was my ticket up to the next floor. From there, I would have to rely on my recall to navigate my way to the right service ladders making my way up the multiple floors.

The longer I sat waiting for the Nano-virus to take effect, the more I rationalized my actions. The thing nagging me the most now was this extremely advanced technology and how Lennox Corp had continued to develop it without outside help. I knew the Nano-tech was doing most of the work now, but in the early phases they had to have tech capable of controlling the Nano-tech until they got it to a stabilized point of self evolution. That was where my questions pushed me. Now that I knew two other corporations existed, I wondered what role they were playing in our lives without our knowledge. I also wondered if they knew the conditions we were living in under the Lennox Corp rule and how they were treating their people. These were all questions I intended to have answered when this was all over. Suddenly it started happening, one person went into violent convulsions, followed by another and another. It was the most disturbing thing I had ever seen as more and more of them began erupting violently. As the convulsions subsided, one person after another expired; I will never forget that image. Just as I had hoped, the barge and its systems began shutting down. I triggered the timer on the explosives. I had 10 minutes to exit the barge and get clear of the blast radius. Hopefully,

Laura stuck around. I wouldn't have blamed her if she left. The last thing she saw was me being sealed into a compact space in which I would surely drown. Deep down, I strongly felt our bond had grown to the point she wouldn't leave me. I absolutely needed to believe that right about now.

I rode the bots service elevator up to the next floor and as I exited, alarms sounded as more and more of the barge's functions were going offline. If I was correct, I needed to take a left and shoot down the corridor to the service elevator on the left wall. The elevator should take me up to the side of the barge from which I needed to exit. As I pushed down the corridor, I could hear a patrol on the move. They were talking fast and panicked about getting off of the barge. No one wanted to be on this thing as the systems were shutting down. They didn't even hear me as I gained ground behind them. We were all heading toward the same ladder. I held back and let the first two get up the ladder. As the third man started up the ladder, I grabbed his leg, yanking him back down the rungs breaking his jaw on the way down. Once he hit the ground, I stomped on his throat finishing the job. I took his knife and his fast repeating assault rifle. I climbed up the ladder and shot the other two in the back as they scurried away. I now had to cross about 60 feet to another ladder on the east side of this wing and that would take me all the way to level 5 where I could make my escape. I looked down; I had about 7 minutes. I could see the ladder and I pushed harder and faster than I ever had in my life. I made the climb and saw the outflow pipe. I jumped in and took a fast ride down, shooting out of the side of the ship landing safely in the water. Laura flew up beside me in the boat screaming, "We only have 1 minute, get in". I grabbed onto the side, pulling myself into the boat as she sped away. I looked back and as I did, the explosions had begun, putting on the most amazing pyrotechnics show I had ever seen. I did my best to shield Laura, as the debris rained down from the sky peppering the entire surrounding area. We darted for the edge of the cove. We needed to make the beach on the other side as quickly as possible. It was time to join the assault on the remaining Lennox Corp security force. I continued to watch as the barge crumbled and sank. As I watched, I now knew I had not murdered those people, I had saved them from a fate far worse than death.

We made the bend, and there was our extraction team ready to take us back to the base camp so we could gear up and join the others. We pushed back down the path to the cliffs where our forces had taken position. Among them was Smith, patiently awaiting my return and his next command. I sure was glad to see him. Tim and Riker had taken point with our forces. Smith had done his part, clearing the immediate area of patrols. As expected, the Lennox Corp patrols had flooded the beach, watching in amazement as the barge continued to explode. I ranged out my long rifle at 300 yards and was ready to strike the first blow. There were approximately 200 patrols to our force of 50. We needed to hold the high ground and hit our targets. I combed their ranks, looking for the highest-ranking officer. When I found him, I took him out with one clean shot to the head. That shot signaled the attack, and as he fell to the ground, gunfire rained down from the cliff side. The security patrols scattered like insects when the lights come on. There was no cover to be found; it was a total massacre. After about 5 minutes of shooting, the scores of bodies lay motionless in the sand. We pushed our way to the ocean's front. Any patrols still alive were to be eliminated. I left the clean-up work to the others and returned to base camp. It was time to deliver the victory message on the encrypted network. Tammy and Captain Chip were now clear to deliver the next blows while I got some sleep. Tomorrow, we would all be marching back towards the final elimination of Lennox Corp.

CHAPTER 21

Last Stand

The convoy rolled out early the next morning. High off of our recent victory, everyone was ready to return to S.C. 1 and finish this for good. One of our vehicles had mechanical issues, and it ended up taking us three days to return to S.C. 1. The streets of the S.C. 1 slums were empty when we arrived. Captain Chip and his forces had pushed the patrols into the heart of the city where they had them pinned. Both sides faced heavy resistance. Captain Chip set up a forward operating base a few blocks away from the front line of the push. From my perception things appeared to be at a stalemate. The thing that surprised me, Tammy and the entire force from S.C. 3

had come to here to S.C. 1, though the plan had been to only send a third of the force. Then she and Captain Chip approached me and filled me in on the details. Apparently when Tammy and her forces received the message, they invaded S.C. 3 to find it abandoned. No security, no citizens; a complete ghost town. Tammy concluded that Lennox Corp must have moved their people and resources to S.C. 1, which made sense since the corporate stronghold is based there. Lennox Corp had fortified the interior of S.C.1 with snipers on the rooftops and roving artillery vehicles around the corporate headquarters building. Once the Special Commander went missing, they figured we would come. They must have realized he might break. Considering that we may have infiltrated the hard drive, they figured we would attack the barge first and then come for them. Spread out between the three cities made them vulnerable, so they pooled their resources together at the corporate stronghold to ensure their survival. We didn't have nearly the man power necessary to take on this size of a force. We controlled the outskirts of the city, but they still controlled the interior. But, This was far from over. I needed more information on S.C. 1, so one of Captain Chip's men sent up a digital mapping drone. I wanted a better idea of the layout of the interior of the city. I might uncover a way to breach the corporate building. We still had a chance to avoid full-on confrontation. As we got the drone up into the air, Riker approached and popped off with his usual sarcasm, "Just send that maniac dog in there." He joked. I appeased him with a slight chuckle. I was almost starting to like him, but running intense missions with someone can sometimes have that effect. I also sent two 4 man scout teams into the sewer system to look around. Those runs are like a maze, and finding a path to the corporate building may prove impossible. Time was running out. We needed a way in.

Our position in the city was untenable. At some point, they would push back trying to regain ground. The drone offered a tremendous view of our battleground.   The corporate building had a heavily barricaded single entrance and exit. Down the road, leading to the corporate building, was a tight corridor undoubtedly guarded by snipers. The corporate building itself donned snipers, positioned on its roof. The surrounding buildings were security housing units for on-site security. I found no way to enter from the back. The wall is giant, and wide open sight lines allow the snipers to be vigilant. Even if we broke through the barricades blocking the interior of the city, we had no chance of making it through the tight corridor with the artillery vehicle. These factors made taking a force straight down the road and into the corporate building impossible.

The technician sent up the drone again. This time the drone mapped the area we controlled around the corporate building, prioritizing the highest yet closest structures to the corporate building. When the images returned, I found my answer. On the east side of the corporate building, two streets over, stood an enormous water tower that held the cities reserve in case of emergency. It wasn't close enough to raise any suspicions climbing up on it, but it was close enough that we might find a way over to the corporate building. The risk is high, but I will take it. Laura suggested a harpoon gun, like the one mounted on my buggy. It would be a one shot try, to covering that distance. The firing mechanism should be a small explosive detonation. "Let's give that a try Laura. You can head back and get started," I said. Captain Chip agreed to give her whatever she needed to build the harpoon. I climbed to the top of the water tower for recon and to get a true measurement of the distance, with height factored into the equation. I took my long rifle with me. I needed to count how many snipers occupied that roof. If we intended to use the harpoon, I would need to eliminate the snipers first. The service ladder to the top of the water tower was by far the tallest ladder I had ever climbed; it just kept going. I never liked ladders much. I preferred free climbing a rock face to climbing any ladder. Once I reached the service platform, I laid down. Through my rifle scope, I had a clear look at the rooftop activities. My scope read about 400 meters rooftop to rooftop. That meant 1,200 feet of rope and a harpoon gun strong enough to fire it over that kind of distance; no way. We needed an alternative plan. I needed to return later for more recon work, but for now I needed to hurry back to the forward operating base and tell Laura not to waste the time or the supplies making a harpoon gun. I returned and found Laura already working hard to collect supplies. I sat her down and explained the situation. Though disappointed, she understood that we must scrap the plan. She and I returned to the water tower together that evening to gather any additional information we could by monitoring the activities at the corporate building after dark. We laid on the platform all night, through multiple patrol and sniper changes. I clocked the entire routine of the security team in charge of protecting the building. The top 3 floors were heavily guarded with constant patrols. The top floor, which contained the board members, boasted the highest level of men. Though unable to look into the boardroom from our vantage point, we could surmise the most obvious location. They left the middle floors completely unprotected. This was not too surprising considering the sizable force on the ground level. There appeared to be two artillery vehicles patrolling in a constant circle around the corporate building. They made a loop around the building, and then went down the road and came back, repeatedly. Having followed the routine of the security patrols for many hours, it became clear what my next plan of action would be. There was no way to attack this building with a force our size. My job wasn't to figure out a way to get us all inside; I just needed to get myself inside. The true purpose of the patrols was to act as a deterrent to our forces. They built them to stop an invasion; not one man. With proper preparation and timing, I planned on sneaking in right under their noses. I would need to find a blind spot and scale the building up to one of the unpatrolled floors, entering through a window. Laura picked up I had figured something out. She asked. "What is it? I can tell from that grin, the answer revealed itself to you." I smiled. My time with Laura was becoming more and more meaningful. I answered her, 'Yes it has, and they will never see it coming." I explained to her my plan to enter the building alone and work my way up to the top floor. Although she would rather I didn't go in there alone, she agreed it was by far the best plan, and probably the only plan that stood any actual chance of success. She agreed to be my over watch. She would take up a position on the tower and feed me information on guard movements or any other activity that seemed out of the ordinary or contrary to the routine. We spent two more nights tracking the activities of the security forces before I felt comfortable making my move on the building. They didn't seem like they were preparing any kind of offensive, just trying to wait us out. It didn't matter, the longer we waited the weaker it made us. We couldn't hold them indefinitely.

After our last night of recon I began preparing everything I needed to breach the building and finish this. I had a spear gun and rope, climbing spikes for scaling the side of the building and a glass breaker for the windows. Besides these items I would bring my knives and tomahawk. No guns for this stealth mission. I had to climb up ten floors to reach the unpatrolled area just below the boardroom. The elevator was out of the question. It would immediately alert them to my presence and ruin my chances of getting in that room. So I have to think on the fly once inside and figure out a path to the boardroom. I hope they have a private elevator for board members. Climbing up the elevator's shaft and popping directly into the room would make my day.

I packed up, dressed in my tactical gear and headed for the water tower. I wanted to get one last look at things and get Laura positioned before I made my move. I got her set up on her perch; she brought my long rifle and thermal binoculars. We rigged up a shortwave radio communication with an amplifier on the tower to communicate. After the sniper shift change, I would make my move. This group appeared less aware than the 4 that worked the building ahead of them; the principal reasons I picked such a late time to make my move. Anybody coming on at 3 a.m. was bound to be more tired, plus, I needed the cloak of darkness to scale the building. I made my way through the side streets and around the barricade where I cut a hole in the fence and climbed up onto one of the security housing units. I jumped from one to the next until I neared the building. I shot the spear gun, with the rope attached, up around the tenth floor window. Nailed it! I swung over and sank my climbing spikes into the hard rock of the building. With a solid foothold established, I started my climb to the tenth floor. This was not a strenuous climb compared to others I had done, but the implications if I fell were much greater. I made my way up to the tenth floor with ease, and with two pointed smacks with the glass breaker, the glass shattered. I jumped into the building prepared for action, but to my surprise, nothing. The power struggled to stay on, and so did the technology running the building. Destroying the barge had destroyed Lennox Corp. The board members were just protecting their lives at this point. Their legacy was already dead. This building and their sizeable security force represented their last stand, and it had failed the minute I entered the building.

CHAPTER 22

Mixed Emotions

O nce I entered the building, I began my search for anything that looked like it could be a private elevator shaft. I searched the entire 10th floor, taking advantage of the lack of security presence. The lights constantly flickering on and off didn't help the search go any faster. On top of that, this building was gigantic and searching the entire 10th floor would take longer than I could spare. I found the main elevator shaft. If worse came to worse, I could use it to navigate up to floor 22, the last remaining floor without a security patrol. The power was getting more and more unpredictable as total blackouts became increasingly more frequent, creating an eerie scene throughout. I only had a small pocket light, as I had not anticipated so many issues with the power. I assumed Lennox Corp would have a quality backup power supply, but this place was hanging on by a thread. As I continued to search the 10th floor for any information that would let me get up to that top floor, an alarm sounded. I couldn't tell if they were on to me or if another system failed. I searched the offices and rooms at a furious pace, tearing them apart looking for clues. It seemed a waste of time, so I walked back out to the main elevator shaft and began the climb. With time against me, I made the 23rd floor my target. I had to eliminate the security patrols on floors 23 and 24 to avoid a reunion on the 25th floor. They may hear me coming, but the boardroom would be locked down tight, with all the board members inside, regardless. Maybe I'll find a way in on my way up. I began the climb; 13 floors straight up a shaky elevator shaft in the ever changing lighting conditions. This would be one of the most challenging climbs of my life. I began the climb treating it like any other. I had a saying when I climbed, "Strong grip, strong climb." So I just continued to put one arm past the other, reassuring my grip with each move upward. I found a decent way to create a foothold and relieve the stress from my arms. As I found a groove, I picked up the pace. I could feel it now. The adrenaline built with every floor I passed. Before I knew it, I saw floor 20. I finished the climb and pulled myself up to the opening for floor 23. I nestled into a little perch and gave myself a few seconds to rest. I shook out my arms and legs, took a deep breath and prepared to call Laura. There was a strong possibility that security forces would be right on top of me as soon as I opened the doors. It was time to use my other eyes. I pulled the radio out of my bag and made the call. Laura had been tracking my movement the entire time. She had not lost sight of me until I entered the elevator shaft. She also noticed the blackouts getting worse and lasting longer and longer. I told her what I had to do, and she focused all of her attention on floor 23. She saw about 70 percent of the floor so that gave me eyes in the sky. The rest I could handle on my own. She counted fifteen guards on the twenty third floor divided into three patrols of five. All heavily armed and ready for a fight. She was clocking their routine, and I was happy to wait as I continued to think about the climb. I had now been in the dark for a good ten minutes. At this point the darkness presented me with an advantage. My long rifle had a thermal scope attachment in its case. If Laura engaged the scope, she could spot enemies for me as I made my way through the floors. In theory I would have eyes and they wouldn't. After watching them make their rounds a few times, Laura had them pegged.

The power was still out, and they had resorted to

using tactical flashlights mounted on their weapons. This was an excellent sign: no night vision. If this power outage persisted, my plan wouldn't fail. I pried the doors open slowly, as I waited for Laura to give me the signal. She would tell me immediately after the first patrol passed my position so I could fall in behind them and take them out. I patiently waited, easing the door open only a bit. I wanted to avoid detection as long as possible. I got the word from Laura, they had just passed. I saw their tactical flashlights as they went by. This should go smoothly. The alarms still blared as the electrical systems continued to falter, so the chances were good they didn't realize there was a threat inside of the building. Unfortunately for them, they had the wrong jobs tonight. I moved in behind them quietly. I heard them complaining about the power and having to patrol this same floor over and over again. If they had known I was creeping up right behind them, they may not have wasted their last few words complaining. I pulled out my tomahawk and sliced through them with precision and stealth. All five of them dropped without firing a shot or even as much as letting out a scream. As they hit the floor, Laura keyed up the radio telling me to stay on my current line where I would intersect with the second patrol in 30 feet. As I made my way toward them, I saw their tactical lights as they turned the corner. This unit was moving right toward me. I ducked into an office and waited. Laura let me know when they passed. They would meet with the same fate, hopefully before we reached the site of the next unit. I lay low, and as the patrol passed, one of them broke off and ducked into the office to do a sweep where I was hiding. As he made his way through the office, I patiently waited in a very dark corner, in the back of the office, behind a large rack of supplies. As he made his way to my position, I got one of my throwing knives pre-pared. I would base this throw on the position of his tactical light, aiming for the head and neck area. It would be a tough throw. The light scanned the room, and I waited for my opportunity. Right as the light hit my position I took my throw. It was a direct hit, right to the neck. He was dead before he even knew what hit him. I moved up to check the body. He appeared to be a commander in charge of the units on this floor. I pocketed his ID card and checked in with Laura. We worked our way through the remaining five patrols keeping the disturbance to a minimum. I have always been efficient at killing, but these days I find myself able to eliminate the enemy without becoming injured myself.

Threat eliminated, I did a quick search on this floor for the private elevator; still no luck. Then I came to a locked door at the end of the corridor. I remembered the ID card, pulled it out and swiped it through the reader. The door opened onto an emergency flight of stairs and they appeared to head up to the twenty fifth floor. Before I entered,

Laura began scanning the areas she could see. Unfortunately, the staircase where I had to make my entry, was out of her view. There were 20 heavily armed guards accumulated in front of one room. That had to be where the board members were hiding out. How do you penetrate a guarded fortress?

I sat outside in the stairwell trying to figure out how to get into that room. Then it hit me. I went up the emergency staircase to the top and entered the rooftop through the emergency hatch. I would take out the snipers on the roof and drop into the room from the ventilation duct on the roof. I had Laura scout the sniper locations and get me prepared to move on them. They were wearing night-vision goggles, and I needed to approach them carefully. As I came out onto the roof, Laura guided me to the first sniper perch. I came up behind him, grabbed him by the neck and squeezed until the life expired from his eyes. The patrols were spread out in different directions across the roof. Laura continued to be my other set of eyes. Ever since the power went out, I was noticing my eyes adjusting magnificently to the dark; another Nano-tech adjustment. I can't begin to imagine what else is in store for me.

By the time I took out the last sniper, I was seeing in the dark with near perfect eyesight. I began looking for a ventilation shaft bigger than the rest. That would be the one to take me into the boardroom. If they were going to be held up in there for long periods of time, they needed a larger and more efficient air exchange system for that room. After searching the roof carefully, I decided on a very large vent that still exchanged airflow despite the power outage. This had to be it. I pulled off the cover of the ventilation shaft and slid straight down, smashing through the ceiling and into an empty boardroom. At first I thought for sure I had made a mistake and found myself stuck in a random boardroom. Then out of no-where all the lights came on. I thought for sure it was a tap and they had me. Then suddenly, an image played on the screen in front of me. It was a digital interface message being broadcast live from an outside location.

The image of a well dressed older man came into clear focus. He began to speak, "Hello Tristan." He could read the surprise on my face. "Yes I know who you are. I searched for you for over twenty years to prevent this day from happening and yet here we are. I obviously failed." "Who are you?" I asked him as I took a seat in one of the office chairs. He responded. "I am Arthur Lennox Jr. My father founded Lennox Corp long before the fall of the world or the invention of Nano-tech. My father was an honorable man. Humanitarian-ism was his legacy, but not mine. Mine has always been and always will be Nano-tech. You thought you could burn down Lennox Corp and I will admit, you succeeded from the outside looking in, but I saw you coming before you knew you were coming. We were ready to make our move on the other corporations but too many board members lacked the spine, so I dissolved the board years ago. Lennox Corp is mine and mine alone. You have buried the Lennox Corp name, but you have failed in your ultimate goal; stopping the use and spread of Nano-tech. While your strike on the barge was bold and served its purpose, it was hardly the final blow. The moment I saw the possibility of you destroying everything I built, I began negotiations to sell Nano-tech to the highest bidder, between the competing corporations. I have left this place to complete my business transaction and guarantee the future implementation of Nano-tech in every corporate controlled society. My price has nothing to do with monetary value. I plan to use Nano-tech to buy myself a seat at one of the other corporation's tables, allowing me to keep my position of power and security. I stay

ahead of my opponents and I will always be ahead
of you. Congratulations! You liberated the Wasteland. Little do you and your fellow slum raised
heathens understand, they forced Lennox Corp
into this part of the world because my father was
weak. The world away from this dump is full of
opportunity for a man with my talents and assets.
So, enjoy your victory. You have officially carved
out your corner of freedom in the depths of hell
on earth. If we ever see each other again Tristan,
which is highly unlikely, I can promise you I will
not spare your life. Do not pursue me. Stay in your
part of the world. You earned it!" The broadcast
closed, and that was it.

Lennox Corp was no more, but Nano-tech
and Arthur Lennox lived on. He didn't realize it,
but he had made a crucial mistake letting me
see his face. I now knew exactly who I was looking for and will search the ends of the earth to
find him. I walked right out of the front door of

the boardroom and faced the security patrols. My plan was to show them the empty room and try to make them see that there was no Lennox Corp anymore. No citizens of the city versus citizens of the slums. Just people finally free to choose their own path. I pushed the door open from the inside and there stood an entire force in shock to see the guy they were supposed to be watching for, walking out of the one place he shouldn't be. I raised my hands into the air and pleaded with them to hear me out. I let them put me in restraints and had them walk me into the boardroom where I could show them it was empty. I told them if one of them knew how to playback the latest conversation they could hear the exchange between Arthur Lennox and myself. Unfortunately there was not enough power to generate a playback, so I explained to them the facts. I told them to look around. This had all been a huge lie. If no one was here who were they protecting? If they had been told they were protecting someone, they were putting their lives at risk for a lie. They were beginning to see my point of view. I was completely honest with them about how I entered the premises and how many men I had killed in the within the building and on top of the building. I apologized to anyone that might have been friends with those men, but explained that this was war. Then I said, "The war has ended and we are all free men and women. The time has come for us to learn to coexist in the cities and in the slums. We must rebuild in the people' image of freedom."

The patrols turned themselves over to Captain Chip. He will teach the people how to come together as one. I radioed Laura and told her how the events had played out. She was the only one I planned to tell about Arthur Lennox. The people of the slums needed a definitive win after the effort they put in, risking everything to come together and go against Lennox Corp. The resolution was real; I had liberated the Wasteland and paved the way for the people to pursue a better life. But, the actual threat still existed. I wanted to take pride in the amazing victory but knowing Nano-tech was still out there and possibly being sold into more dangerous hands, left me with mixed emotions.

CHAPTER 23

Unexpected Return

Laura and I returned to the forward operating base and to my surprise my mother was there waiting for me. She signaled me over to her, but I had more pressing matters to attend to so she would have to wait. I sat down with Captain Chip and told him we destroyed Lennox Corp and the remaining security force wants to make a deal. I didn't know where the citizens of the city were being held, but I would soon find out. Captain Chip would be the perfect person to sit down with the security patrols and negotiate the terms of their surrender. He worked closely with Lennox Corp for many years and should be familiar with many of the men. I told him I wanted nothing to do with the process, my path would lead me elsewhere. He agreed and took a security detail with him to the interior of the city to meet with the highest ranking member of the security team. Meanwhile, I headed back to the slums of S.C. 1 to find my mother and have a talk. We found a nice bench in a quiet area of the square and took a seat. She started the conversation with a question as she often did, "Did you eliminate Lennox Corp?" Somehow she already seemed apprised that Arthur Lennox took his leave some time back. I answered her. "Yes, but I may have created an even bigger threat." I filled her in on my conversation with Arthur Lennox and his claim to be selling Nano-tech for a seat on the board of one of the other corporations. "You still don't understand, do you?" she asked. I grew tired of her games and wanted answers. "It seems I'm missing something, why don't you fill me in." She explained, "I surmise that Arthur Lennox is cleaning house. The information I gained from my contact in S.C. 3 led me to conclude Arthur Lennox is the puppet master of the entire operation. By that I'm talking he manipulated all the pieces on the board, purposely orchestrating the downfall of Lennox Corp. He never liked the piece of the world his father settled for and his ambitions leaned towards acquiring more power and status." Her belief was they finally perfected Nano-tech and planned to use it not to take over the other corporations, but to have power over and to control them. Her source convinced her Lennox' goal was to sell the other corporations tainted versions of Nano-tech that he alone could secretly control and manipulate.

It made sense now. Arthur Lennox laid out all the bread crumbs that put me on the trail to taking down Lennox Corp. He needed everyone with knowledge about Nano-tech and how to develop it removed from the equation, but could never do it himself. He needed someone from the outside creating an uprising of the people, ultimately keeping his hands clean. His story of losing his empire would also serve as a tool of fear that would drive the other corporations straight to him for Nano-tech to control their empires. Lennox Corp reached its maximum potential, and no longer had the technology or manpower to continue progressing Nano-tech. He's been planning a rather unique takeover of the other corporations. He wasn't building an army, he was destroying the evidence. This was incredible. Then I asked my mother, "What makes any of this true?" She said, "Nothing, but the pieces are all there and when I arrived in S.C.3, my friend told me they were preparing for and evacuation through the emergency tunnel. When I asked her where they were to go, she said that all citizens were being moved to S.C.2 and all security forces were being reassigned to guard the corporate building in S.C. 1. That is when I knew that S.C. 1 was a diversion to cover his escape. If protecting his legacy took precedence, he would have diverted all the security forces to the barge. I knew S.C. 2 would be unguarded, so that is where I headed when I left. I hoped to gain the support of the citizens for our cause. But when I arrived, they had destroyed the entire city with the citizens inside. I arrived too late, everyone had perished. When I saw S.C. 2 in ashes still smoldering, I became sure they had played us. I tried to get back to S.C. 1 to warn you of the diversion and probable trap, but when I arrived, Captain Chip told me you had already gone into the interior of the city with intentions of entering the corporate building. I did not discern he had dissolved the board. No wonder no one ever saw them anymore". It appeared my mother was correct. Finally, all the pieces came together. Arthur Lennox was a high stakes player and had reached his ceiling with Lennox Corp. I played right into his hands and though our corner of the world was safe for now, the fate of the entire world outside of here appeared to be in grave jeopardy. There are no actions in this world free from consequences, and it is the unforseen that always pose the biggest threat.

I asked my mother if she would help Captain Chip get a good hold on things now that the cities would merge with the slums. There would be many people who would try to take advantage of a situation like this and seize power. It would be their job to make sure that didn't happen. I also needed another favor from her. I needed her to prepare a file for me containing everything she could pull together about the world beyond ours and any information she possessed about the other corporations operating in the world. She agreed, but I saw in her eyes she still had something more to tell me. She looked me dead in the eyes and said, "I have to warn you before you walk this path, that the last I heard from Kalil he was working freelance for Bliskin Corp trying to earn their trust. "Kalil was convinced they were developing the next level of community control and somehow Lennox Corp was involved." The revelations just kept coming. There was an actual possibility that Kalil was still alive and that I might see him again someday. This was the first piece of positive news I had heard since my mother's return. She told me she would put together all the information that Kalil had passed along to her and make it available to me.

Even though I had not fully completed my mission, this experience taught me my place and purpose in this world. I would expose the corruption and end the tyranny for all people of this world and any world beyond it. I would not lie down in the face of danger or turn a blind eye. I would make it my mission to succeed where others failed and create a new world free of the chains that bind our hands and our choices. My mother chronicled all the information she could recall about the other corporations and the world beyond the Wasteland. It wasn't much. She had

never left our piece of the world and her interactions with other corporations was even more
limited as Lennox Corp had been isolating themselves for decades while testing on their citizens
and developing Nano-tech.

I found Laura and told her I was heading out
to my mother's for a few days and I would meet
her back at S.C. 3 when I returned. I enjoyed a
few days with my mother out at her cabin in the
Wasteland, as she talked about what would need
to be done to bring the communities together,
and gathered the materials I had requested. As I
watched her move about, it continued to be hard
to believe she was my mother, and I still wasn't
sure how I felt about being conceived to become
a Savior. But I learned a lot about myself with my
mother's help and in my heart I would miss her.
We enjoyed a tea on the porch one more time before it was time to go. As I went to thank her, she
put her arms around me and said, "I'm so proud

of the man you have become and of what you did for the people. I have no doubts this is your true path, son. I do love you." I was left speechless. I leaned down, kissing her on her forehead, turned and headed for the slums.

Once back in the slums of S.C. 3, I sought out Laura and Smith. She and Smith had been gathering supplies and things we may need. They both greeted me like they hadn't seen me for weeks. After a few minutes, Laura asked, "What did you talk about with your mother? You look rattled." I replied, "That is for another time. We will have plenty of time to discuss everything on our journey." She and I headed back to my bunker and prepare for the road trip ahead. We both knew that we had an unfamiliar world of adventures waiting on us, and the times ahead of were sure to carry an unfamiliar weight from the dreams we once knew. Somehow, we both realized this was the life we were to live from now on. This was the path our destiny had put us on and we intended to walk it to its fullest extent. From the first moment we met at the blacksmith shop, our lives became inexplicably entwined and we would now take the adventures ahead together; Me, Laura and Smith.

CHAPTER 24

Goodbye to the Wasteland

Laura and I spent the next few weeks in my bunker going over the information my mother provided me. Clarity Corp another extension of Bliskin Corp and apparently reserved for all the most important and highest level contributors to their multi-level society. Clarity Corp had the responsibility of maintaining the technology for the Bliskin Corporations bigger manufacturing operations. As long as they provided service and Labor to Bliskin Corp they could operate freely and primarily govern on their own terms. According to my mother's files, everyone living under the control of the Clarity Corp lives a life of excess and abundance. Clarity Corp used material possession and inclusion to manipulate their society. They pretended to be independent, but in reality nothing they did could be free from the rule of Bliskin Corp when it all came down to it. She could supply me almost no information on Bliskin Corp, only that they were the largest corporation to survive the fall, and they made their name in the world producing weapons of mass destruction for the highest bidding government. After combing over the notes for weeks and also taking a little time to relax after the recent events, we both became stir crazy. We had a mission and it would not fulfill itself. Plus, I think the more time that Laura and I spent together the more we sensed ourselves falling in love, and I don't think either of us were ready to deal with that level of emotions. We needed an adventure to channel that energy.

According to the maps I made of the Waste-land over the years, and my mother's knowledge of the world beyond the Wasteland, our journey would bring us into Clarity Corp territory first. There only workable way to make it out of the Wasteland involved a trip through the drought-stricken No-man's-land, considered by all to be impossible to cross. Laura and I would need to pack our vehicle wisely and be sure we packed everything we might need to survive the trip. Even if I couldn't die of dehydration, Laura sure could. We could not afford to get lost. There was the possibility of magnetic interference that would render compasses useless, so we would need to travel by night with the stars as our guide. That would work out best anyway, considering the heat during the day. The excitement between us was unmistakable as we spent the next few days gathering and loading supplies. Even Smith got in on the excitement, bringing along his favorite chew toys.

We made a plan to head out the next morning, when we were both convinced we packed everything we would need. That would put us making it to No-man's-land by nightfall, giving us an entire first night of travel before we would set up camp in No-man's-land. I eventually planned to tell her everything about me, but for now we both had been through so much that I felt better dispensing it to her in small doses. It likely would be a lot for a normal person to wrap their head around. We spent the entire day travelling and as we did; I found myself reminiscing. I wasn't reminiscing on the events of recent, instead my mind carried me back to the adventures I experienced in the Wasteland, before I found my true purpose in life. Even though I now had a purpose and a mission, a part of me missed my simple care free life of scavenging and exploring the Wasteland. The world seemed a much simpler place when I thought I was just some mutant freak destined to wander the Wasteland, accepting the Wasteland as my entire world. I had never even dreamed of anything beyond the Wasteland. I was so mad at Kalil when he went off to explore the world beyond the Wasteland. I didn't believe there was anything out there, and I thought he was abandoning me. I now realized that my entire world had been a lie and that wherever Kalil had gone, he went there to save the world, the entire world. I was taken in by the lies told by Lennox Corp just as so many others were and I now grasped the truth: there was a vast world beyond the Wasteland. What I didn't know was what exactly that world may hold for Laura and I once we found it.

The ride to the edge of no-man's-land was a quiet one. Laura saw that I had a lot on my mind and left me to my introspection. I imagine she was probably doing some reflection of her own. We reached the edge of no-man's-land just before nightfall just as we planned. But instead of proceeding, we set up camp and called it a day. I expect both of us needed a little more time to sever the cord between the life we knew and the world that lay beyond. We sat up all night, looking at the stars and sharing stories about the blacksmith and others we had called friends. Both of us recognized we may never return to the Wasteland and wanted to cherish the memories created there. The more we talked, the more our emotions and feelings came rushing back. Laura and I could no longer hide our true feelings for one another. All the weeks pinned up in the bunker together we denied our feelings, but on this night under the stars all of that changed. We had committed ourselves on every level. We were no longer just on a mission together we were moving forward with our lives together. This was a huge turning point for both of us. We had both lived a solitary life filled with day-to-day tasks but little meaning. Now we would have the opportunity to experience the joys, the tears, the excitement of a life; sharing it with someone, giving it meaning together. She finally fell asleep, nestled up close to me as the sun peaked over the horizon. As I felt its warm glow on my face, true peace came over me for the first time in my entire life. I let my eyes fade closed, as I pulled Laura in even closer to me. We slept throughout the entire day until around dusk. We ate a solid meal before packing up our camp and while waiting for the sun to fall out of sight. As the sun gave way, and the stars revealed themselves, I turned taking one last look at the Wasteland behind us. The time had come to say goodbye. Although the odds said it was unlikely we would ever return to the Wasteland, I had spent my entire life defying the odds and something told me I would one day return. And even though this was goodbye for now it would not be goodbye forever.

ACKNOWLEDGE-MENTS

F irst of all I would like to thank my support system. Due to the private nature of my life and out of respect for the privacy of those who have contributed to this project I would just like to say nothing in this world is done without a solid team around you and I want to express my deepest gratitude to everyone who contributed to the conception of this book. Next I would like to thank all of you, the readers. This is my first book of many and I look forward to not only growing the story and characters involved, but also expanding my own personal writing skills and with your support I know anything is possible. Last of all I would like to acknowledge the universal energy that drives and connects all of us. Without my belief in something bigger driving us all, I would not be able to tap into my full potential and become the creator of such complex and genuine characters and worlds. Thank you all for your support and I look forward to sharing future successes with you as we take this journey together.

ABOUT THE AUTHOR

Mark Browning

Mark Browning is a creator of worlds, writing everything from poetry to creative works of fiction. Wielding the pen like a mighty sword, using intellect over force, he is always looking to push the limits of thought and the way we see the world we live in. With a background in creative writing and contributions to several music projects, his range and scale resonate over multiple demographics. As an only child from a small town, a bold imagination and amazing eye for detail emerged at an early age. Ultimately, story-telling and writing became a driving force for everything in his life. The need to create resonates from deep within in an effort to leave the readers with not only questions they may not have thought to ask, but also the confidence and perspective to see the answers that may not have been clear to them previously. He sums his writing up by saying "Creation is always more difficult than destruction if we allow it to be, but creation is so much more powerful when it is the driving force behind change".

www.ingramcontent.com/pod-product-compliance
Lightning Source LLC
Chambersburg PA
CBHW031703170626
46808CB00005B/1592